HE HAS SOARED ON THE WINGS OF OUR DREAMS AND PLUMBED THE DEPTHS OF OUR NIGHTMARES.

Amid the pastoral beauty of America's South, John the wanderer charts a nomad's trail. Some of his journeys have led him to hell's door.

There he has seen the hoodoo man and the fearful bird that inhabits the dark side of the soul. There he has stalked the Kalu, the cursed thing that eats whatever—or whomever—it finds. He has been face to face with the One Other who, with but one arm and leg, drags his victims down into the Bottomless Pool. He has sought the golden treasure of Blake Pine Hollow, where "the sun never shines."

He has risked countless terrors, but each time he has come back alive—yearning to travel, to venture on. . . .

THE BEST IN CONTEMPORARY FANTASY FROM DELL

THE DOOR INTO FIRE Diane Duane
*LAND OF UNREASON L. Sprague de Camp and Fletcher Pratt
*SLAVES OF SLEEP L. Ron Hubbard
MASTER OF HAWKS Linda E. Bushyager
*DARKER THAN YOU THINK Jack Williamson
THE ETERNAL CHAMPION Michael Moorcock
ANOTHER FINE MYTH Robert Asprin
RENEGADE OF CALLISTO Lin Carter
*FLASHING SWORDS! #4: BARBARIANS AND BLACK MAGICIANS
Lin Carter, editor
THE SILVER WARRIORS Michael Moorcock
WALL OF SERPENTS L. Sprague de Camp and Fletcher Pratt
*HASAN Piers Anthony
*THE FORTUNES OF BRAK John Jakes

*denotes an illustrated book

WHO FEARS THE DEVIL?

Manly Wade Wellman

A DELL BOOK

Published by
Dell Publishing Co., Inc.
1 Dag Hammarskjold Plaza
New York, New York 10017

O Ugly Bird!, copyright 1946 by Fantasy House, Inc., for *The Magazine of Fantasy and Science-Fiction*, December 1951.

The Desrick on Yandro, copyright 1952 by Fantasy House, Inc., for *The Magazine of Fantasy and Science-Fiction*, June 1952.

Vandy, Vandy, copyright 1953 by Fantasy House, Inc., for *The Magazine of Fantasy and Science-Fiction*, March 1953.

One Other, copyright 1953 by Fantasy House, Inc., for *The Magazine of Fantasy and Science-Fiction*, August 1953.

Dumb Supper (original title *Call Me from the Valley*). copyright 1954 by Fantasy House, Inc., for *The Magazine of Fantasy and Science-Fiction*, March 1954.

The Little Black Train, copyright 1954 by Fantasy House, Inc., for *The Magazine of Fantasy and Science-Fiction*, August 1954.

Shiver in the Pines, copyright 1955 by Fantasy House, Inc., for *The Magazine of Fantasy and Science-Fiction*, February 1955.

Walk Like a Mountain, copyright 1955 by Fantasy House, Inc., for *The Magazine of Fantasy and Science-Fiction*, June 1955.

On the Hills and Everywhere, copyright 1956 by Fantasy House, Inc., for *The Magazine of Fantasy and Science-Fiction*, January 1956.

Old Devlins Was A-Waiting, copyright 1957 by Fantasy House, Inc., for *The Magazine of Fantasy and Science-Fiction*, February 1957.

Nine Yards of Other Cloth, copyright 1958 by Mercury Press, Inc., for *The Magazine of Fantasy and Science-Fiction*, July 1958.

Why They're Named That, Then I Wasn't Alone, You Know the Tale of Hoph, The Stars Down There, Blue Monkey, I Can't Claim That and *Who Else Could I Count On?* (Collected Under title *Wonder as I Wander*) copyright 1962 by Mercury Press, Inc., for *The Magazine of Fantasy and Science Fiction*, March 1962.

Copyright © 1963 by Manly Wade Wellman
Illustrations copyright © 1980 by Tim Kirk

All rights reserved. No part of this book may be reproduced or transmitted in any form or by any means, electronic or mechanical, including photocopying, recording or by any information storage and retrieval system, without the written permission of the Publisher, except where permitted by law. For information address Arkham House Publishers, Inc., Sauk City, Wisconsin.

Dell ® TM 681510, Dell Publishing Co., Inc.

ISBN: 0-440-19776-7

Reprinted by arrangement with Arkham House Publishers, Inc.
Printed in the United States of America
First Dell printing—February 1980

ACKNOWLEDGMENTS

Except for a few of the shorter sketches, all these stories appeared in somewhat different form in *The Magazine of Fantasy and Science-Fiction,* over a period of nearly a dozen years. Grateful acknowledgment is made to the publisher for permission to reprint them for this book.

And I venture to offer affectionate thanks to those proud, warmhearted and mannerly men and women of the North Carolina mountains, among whom I once came as a stranger and to whom I return again and again as a friend; who made me welcome to their firesides and tables, who sang me songs and told me tales; who, as I hope, will read the truth of their own lives in these written memories of strange things I have heard in the shadows of their tall rocks, beside their bright waters, among their green trees. Nobly and naturally, these people match their own mountains.

—Manly Wade Wellman
Chapel Hill, North Carolina
January 1, 1963

Dedicated
with admiration and affection
to
*Obray and Beillie,
Bascom and Freda,
Don and Edna,
Byard, Doward, Marvin,
The Hunters, the Fishers,
and all the other natural men and women—my friends,
making their last stand for being natural, among
the high hills and deep hollows*

*... High on the top of the mountain,
Away from the sins of this world. ...*

> Who fears the Devil?
>   says Jane unto Jim,
> Who fears the Devil?
>   says Jim unto Joan,
> Who fears the Devil?
>   says Joan unto John—
>   Not I! Not I!
>   says John all alone.

—from a game song, once popular with Southern children

CONTENTS

John's My Name O UGLY BIRD!	13
Why They're Named That ONE OTHER	35
Then I Wasn't Alone SHIVER IN THE PINES	57
You Know the Tale of Hoph OLD DEVLINS WAS A-WAITING	81
Find the Place Yourself THE DESRICK ON YANDRO	107
The Stars Down There VANDY, VANDY	125
Blue Monkey DUMB SUPPER	145
I Can't Claim That THE LITTLE BLACK TRAIN	161
Who Else Could I Count On? WALK LIKE A MOUNTAIN	181
None Wiser for the Trip ON THE HILLS AND EVERYWHERE	203
Nary Spell NINE YARDS OF OTHER CLOTH	215

JOHN'S MY NAME

Where I've been is places and what I've seen is things, and there've been times I've run off from seeing them, off to other places and things. I keep moving, me and this guitar with the silver strings to it, slung behind my shoulder. Sometimes I've got food with me and an extra shirt maybe, but most times just the guitar, and trust to God for what I need else.

I don't claim much. John's my name, and about that I'll only say I hope I've got some of the goodness of good men who've been named it. I'm no more than just a natural man; well, maybe taller than some. Sure enough, I fought in the war across the sea, but so does near about every man in war times. Now I go here and go there, and up and down, from place to place and from thing to thing, here in among the mountains.

Up these heights and down these hollows you'd best go expecting anything. Maybe everything. What's long time ago left off happening outside still goes on here, and the tales the mountain folks tell sound truer here than outside. About what I tell, if you believe it you might could get some good thing out of it. If you don't believe it, well, I don't have a gun out to you to make you stop and hark at it.

O UGLY BIRD!

I swear I'm licked before I start, trying to tell you all what Mr. Onselm looked like. Words give out sometimes. The way you're purely frozen to death for fit words to tell the favor of the girl you love. And Mr. Onselm and I pure poison hated each other from the start. That's a way that love and hate are alike.

He's what folks in the country call a low man, meaning he's short and small. But a low man is low other ways than in inches, sometimes. Mr. Onselm's shoulders didn't wide out as far as his big ears, and they sank and sagged. His thin legs bowed in at the knee and out at the shank, like two sickles put point to point. His neck was as thin as a carrot, and on it his head looked like a swollen-up pale gourd. Thin hair, gray as tree moss. Loose mouth, a little bit open to show long, straight teeth. Not much chin. The right eye squinted, mean and dark, while the hike of his brow stretched the left one wide open. His good clothes fitted his mean body as if they were cut to its measure. Those good clothes of his were almost as much out of match to the rest of him as his long, soft, pink hands, the hands of a man who'd never had to work a tap's worth.

You see now what I mean? I can't say just how he looked, only that he looked hateful.

I first met him when I was coming down from that high mountain's comb, along an animal trail—maybe a deer made it. I was making to go on across the valley and through a pass, on to Hark Mountain where I'd heard tell was the Bottomless Pool. No special reason, just I had the notion to go there. The valley had trees in it, and through and among the trees I saw, here and there down the slope, patchy places and cabins and yards.

I hoped to myself I might could get fed at one of the cabins, for I'd run clear out of eating some spell back. I didn't have any money, nary coin of it; just only my hickory shirt and blue jeans pants and torn old army shoes, and my guitar on its sling cord. But I knew the mountain folks. If they've got anything to eat, a decent-spoken stranger can get the half part of it. Town folks ain't always the same way about that.

Down the slope I picked my way, favoring the guitar just in case I slipped and fell down, and in an hour I'd made it to the first patch. The cabin was two rooms, dog-trotted and open through the middle. Beyond it was a shed and a pigpen. In the yard was the man of the house, talking to who I found out later was Mr. Onselm.

"You don't have any meat at all?" Mr. Onselm inquired him, and Mr. Onselm's voice was the last you'd expect his sort of man to have, it was full of broad low music, like an organ in a big town church. But I decided not to ask him to sing when I'd taken another closer glimpse of him—sickle-legged and gourd-headed, and pale and puny in his fine-fitting clothes. For, small as he was, he looked mad and dangerous; and the man of the place, though he was a big, strong-seeming old gentleman with a square jaw, looked scared.

"I been right short this year, Mr. Onselm," he said, and it was a half-begging way he said it. "The last bit of meat I done fished out of the brine on Tuesday. And I'd sure enough rather not to kill the pig till December."

Mr. Onselm tramped over to the pen and looked in. The pig was a friendly-acting one; it reared up with its front feet against the boards and grunted up, the way you'd know he hoped for something nice to eat. Mr. Onselm spit into the pen.

"All right," he said, granting a favor. "But I want some meal."

He sickle-legged back toward the cabin. A brown barrel stood out in the dog trot. Mr. Onselm flung off the cover and pinched up some meal between the tips of his pink fingers. "Get me a sack," he told the man.

The man went quick indoors, and quick out he came, with the sack. Mr. Onselm held it open while the man scooped out enough meal to fill it up. Then Mr. Onselm twisted the neck tight shut and the man lashed the neck with twine. Finally Mr. Onselm looked up and saw me standing there with my guitar under my arm.

"Who are you?" he asked, sort of crooning.

"My name's John," I said.

"John what?" Then he never waited for me to tell him John what. "Where did you steal that guitar?"

"This was given to me," I replied him. "I strung it with the silver wires myself."

"Silver," said Mr. Onselm, and he opened his squint eye by a trifle bit.

"Yes sir." With my left hand I clamped a chord. With my right thumb I picked the silver string to a whisper. I began to make up a song:

> "Mister Onselm,
> They do what you tell 'em—"

"That will do," said Mr. Onselm, not so singingly, and I stopped with the half-made-up song. He relaxed and let his eye go back to a squint again.

"They do what I tell 'em," he said, halfway to himself. "Not bad."

We studied each other, he and I, for a few ticks of time. Then he turned away and went tramping out of the yard and off among the trees. When he was gone from sight, the man of the house asked me, right friendly enough, what he could do for me.

"I'm just a-walking through," I said. I didn't want to ask him right off for some dinner.

"I heard you name yourself John," he said. "Just so happens my name's John, too. John Bristow."

"Nice place you got here, Mr. Bristow," I said, looking around. "You cropping or you renting?"

"I own the house and the land," he told me, and I was surprised; for Mr. Onselm had treated him the way a meanminded boss treats a cropper.

"Oh," I said, "then that Mr. Onselm was just a visitor."

"Visitor?" Mr. Bristow snorted out the word. "He visits ary living soul here around. Lets them know what thing he wants, and they pass it to him. I kindly thought you knew him, you sang about him so ready."

"Oh, I just got that up." I touched the silver strings again. "Many a new song comes to me, and I just sing it. That's my nature."

"I love the old songs better," said Mr. Bristow, and smiled; so I sang one:

"I had been in Georgia
Not a many more weeks than three
When I fell in love with a pretty fair girl
And she fell in love with me.

"Her lips were red as red could be,
Her eyes were brown as brown,
Her hair was like a thundercloud
Before the rain comes down."

Gentlemen, you'd ought to been there, to see Mr. Bristow's face shine. He said: "By God, John, you sure enough can sing it and play it. It's a pure pleasure to hark at you."

"I do my possible best," I said. "But Mr. Onselm doesn't like it." I thought for a moment, then I inquired him: "What's the way he can get ary thing he wants in this valley?"

"Shoo, can't tell you what way. Just done it for years, he has."

"Doesn't anybody refuse him?"

"Well, it's happened. Once, they say, Old Jim Desbro refused him a chicken. And Mr. Onselm pointed his finger at Old Jim's mules, they was a-plowing at the time. Them mules couldn't move nary hoof, not till Mr. Onselm had the chicken from Old Jim. Another time there was, Miss Tilly Parmer hid a cake she'd just baked when she seen Mr. Onselm a-coming. He pointed a finger and he dumbed her. She never spoke one mumbling word from that day on to the day she laid down and died. Could hear and know what was said to her, but when she tried to talk she could only just gibble."

"Then he's a hoodoo man," I said. "And that means, the law can't do a thing to him."

"No sir, not even if the law worried itself up about anything going on this far from the county seat." He looked at the meal sack, still standing in the dogtrot. "Near about time for the Ugly Bird to come fetch Mr. Onselm's meal."

"What's the Ugly Bird?" I asked, but Mr. Bristow didn't have to tell me that.

It must have been a-hanging up there over us, high and quiet, and now it dropped down into the yard, like a fish hawk into a pond.

First out I could see it was dark, heavy-winged, bigger by right much than a buzzard. Then I made out the shiny gray-black of the body, like wet slate, and how the body looked to be naked, how it seemed there were feathers only on the wide wings. Then I saw the long thin snaky neck and the bulgy head and the long crane beak. And I saw the two eyes set in the front of the head—set man-fashion in the front, not bird-fashion one on each side.

The feet grabbed for the sack and taloned onto it,

and they showed pink and smooth, with five grabby toes on each one. Then the wings snapped, like a tablecloth in a high wind, and it went churning up again, and way over the tops of the trees, taking the sack of meal with it.

"That's the Ugly Bird," said Mr. Bristow to me, so low I could just about hear him. "Mr. Onselm's been companioning with it ever since I could recollect."

"Such a sort of bird I never before saw," I said. "Must be a right scarced-out one. Do you know what struck me while I was a-watching it?"

"Most likely I do know, John. It's got feet look like Mr. Onselm's hands."

"Could it maybe be," I asked, "that a hoodoo man like Mr. Onselm knows what way to shape himself into a bird thing?"

But Mr. Bristow shook his gray head. "It's known that when he's at one place, the Ugly Bird's been sighted at another." He tried to change the subject. "Silver strings on your guitar; I never heard tell of aught but steel strings."

"In the olden days," I told him, "silver was used a many times for strings. It gives a more singy sound."

In my mind I had it made sure that the subject wasn't going to be changed. I tried a chord on my guitar, and began to sing:

> "You all have heard of the Ugly Bird
> So curious and so queer,
> It flies its flight by day and night
> And fills folks' hearts with fear."

"John—" Mr. Bristow began to butt in. But I sang on:

> "I never came here to hide from fear,
> And I give you my promised word

That I soon expect to twist the neck
Of the God damn Ugly Bird."

Mr. Bristow looked sick at me. His hand trembled as it felt in his pocket.

"I wish I could bid you stop and eat with me," he said, "but—here, maybe you better buy you something."

What he gave me was a quarter and a dime. I near about gave them back, but I saw he wanted me to have them. So I thanked him kindly and walked off down the same trail through the trees Mr. Onselm had gone. Mr. Bristow watched me go, looking shrunk up.

Why had my song scared him? I kept singing it:

"O Ugly Bird! O Ugly Bird!
You spy and sneak and thieve!
This place can't be for you and me,
And one of us got to leave."

Singing, I tried to recollect all I'd heard or read or guessed that might could help toward studying out what the Ugly Bird was.

Didn't witch folks have partner animals? I'd read, and I'd heard tell, about the animals called familiars. Mostly they were cats or black dogs or such matter as that, but sometimes they were birds.

That might could be the secret, or a right much of it. For the Ugly Bird wasn't Mr. Onselm, changed by witching so he could fly. Mr. Bristow had said the two of them were seen different places at one and the same time. So Mr. Onselm could no way turn himself into the Ugly Bird. They were close partners, no more. Brothers. With the Ugly Bird's feet looking like Mr. Onselm's hands.

I was ware of something up in the sky, the big black V of something that flew. It quartered over me, half as high as the highest scrap of woolly white cloud.

Once or twice it made a turn, seemingly like wanting to stoop for me like a hawk for a rabbit; but it didn't do any such. Looking up at it and letting my feet find the trail on their own way, I rounded a bunch of mountain laurel and there, on a rotten log in the middle of a clearing, sat Mr. Onselm.

His gourd head was sunk down on his thin neck. His elbows set on his crooked knees, and the soft, pink, long hands hid his face, as if he felt miserable. The look of him made me feel disgusted. I came walking close to him.

"You don't feel so brash, do you?" I asked him.

"Go away," he sort of gulped, soft and tired and sick.

"What for?" I wanted to know. "I like it here." Sitting on the log next to him, I pulled my guitar across me. "I feel like singing, Mr. Onselm."

I made it up again, word by word as I sang it:

"His father got hung for hog stealing,
His mother got burnt for a witch,
And his only friend is the Ugly Bird,
The dirty son—"

Something hit me like a shooting star, a-slamming down from overhead.

It hit my back shoulder, and it knocked me floundering forward on one hand and one knee. It was only the mercy of God I didn't fall on my guitar and smash it. I crawled forward a few quick scrambles and made to get up again, shaky and dizzy, to see what had happened.

I saw. The Ugly Bird had flown down and dropped the sack of meal on me. Now it skimmed across the clearing, at the height of the low branches. Its eyes glinted at me, and its mouth came open like a pair of scissors. I saw teeth, sharp and mean, like the teeth of agar fish. Then the Ugly Bird swooped for me, and the wind of its wings was colder than a winter tempest storm.

Without thinking or stopping to think, I flung up my both hands to box it off from me, and it gave back, it flew back from me like the biggest, devilishest humming bird you'd ever see in a nightmare. I was too dizzy and scared to wonder why it pulled off like that; I had barely the wit to be glad it did.

"Get out of here," moaned Mr. Onselm, not stirring from where he sat.

I take shame to say, I got. I kept my hands up and backed across the clearing and to the trail on the far side. Then I halfway thought I knew where my luck had come from. My hands had lifted my guitar up as the Ugly Bird flung itself at me, and some way it hadn't liked the guitar.

Reaching the trail again, I looked back. The Ugly Bird was perching on the log where I'd been sitting. It slaunched along close to Mr. Onselm, sort of nuzzling up to him. Horrible to see, I'll be sworn. They were sure enough close together. I turned and stumbled off away, along the trail down the valley and off toward the pass beyond the valley.

I found a stream, with stones making steps across it. I followed it down to where it made a wide pool. There I got on my knee and washed my face—it looked pale as clabber in the water image—and sat down with my back to a tree and hugged my guitar and had a rest.

I was shaking all over. I must have felt near about as bad for a while as Mr. Onselm had looked to feel, sitting on that rotten log to wait for his Ugly Bird and—what else?

Had he been hungry near to death? Sick? Or maybe had his own evil set back on him? I couldn't rightly say which.

But after a while I felt some better. I got up and walked back to the trail and along it again, till I came to what must have been the only store thereabouts.

It faced one way on a rough gravelly road that could carry wagon traffic, car traffic too if you didn't mind your car getting a good shakeup, and the trail joined on there, right across from the doorway. The building wasn't big but it was good, made of sawed planks, and there was paint on it, well painted on. Its bottom rested on big rocks instead of posts, and it had a roofed open front like a porch, with a bench in there where folks could sit.

Opening the door, I went in. You'll find many such stores in back country places through the land, where folks haven't built their towns up too close. Two-three counters. Shelves of cans and packages. Smoked meat hung up in one corner, a glass-fronted icebox for fresh meat in another. Barrels here and there, for beans or meal or potatoes. At the end of one counter, a sign says U. S. POST OFFICE, and there's a set of maybe half a dozen pigeonholes to put letters in, and a couple of cigar boxes for stamps and money order blanks. That's the kind of place it was.

The proprietor wasn't in just then. Only a girl, scared and shaky back of the counter, and Mr. Onselm, there ahead of me, a-telling her what it was he wanted.

He wanted her.

"I don't care a shuck if Sam Heaver did leave you in charge here," he said with the music in his voice. "He won't stop my taking you with me."

Then he heard me come in, and he swung round and fixed his squint eye and his wide-open eye on me, like two mismated gun muzzles. "You again," he said.

He looked right hale and hearty again. I strayed my hands over the guitar's silver strings, just enough to hear, and he twisted up his face as if it colicked him.

"Winnie," he told the girl, "wait on this stranger and get him out of here."

Her round eyes were scared in her scared face. I thought inside myself that seldom I'd seen as sweet a face as hers, or as scared a one. Her hair was dark and thick. It was like the thundercloud before the rain comes down. It made her paleness look paler. She was small and slim, and she cowered there, for fear of Mr. Onselm and what he'd been saying to her.

"Yes, sir?" she said to me, hushed and shaky.

"A box of crackers, please, ma'am," I decided, pointing to where they were on the shelf behind her. "And a can of those little sardine fish."

She put them on the counter for me. I dug out the quarter Mr. Bristow had given me up the trail, and slapped it down on the counter top between the scared girl and Mr. Onselm.

"Get away!" he squeaked, shrill and sharp and mean as a bat. When I looked at him, he'd jumped back, almost halfway across the floor from the counter. And for just once, his both eyes were big and wide.

"Why, Mr. Onselm, what's the matter?" I wondered him, and I purely was wondering. "This is a good quarter."

I picked it up and held it out for him to take and study.

But he flung himself around, and he ran out of that store like a rabbit. A rabbit with dogs running it down.

The girl he'd called Winnie just leaned against the wall as if she was bone tired. I asked her: "Why did he light out like that?"

I gave her the quarter, and she took it. "That money isn't a scary thing, is it?" I asked.

"It doesn't much scare me," she said, and rang it up on the old cash register. "All that scares me is— Mr. Onselm."

I picked up the box of crackers and sardines. "Is he courting you?"

She shivered, although it was warm in the store. "I'd sooner be in a hole with a snake than be courted by Mr. Onselm."

"Then why not just tell him to leave you be?"

"He wouldn't hark at that," she said. "He always just does what pleasures him. Nobody dares to stop him."

"So I've heard tell," I nodded. "About the mules he stopped where they stood, and the poor old lady he struck dumb." I returned to the other thing we'd been talking. "But what made him squinch away from that money piece? I'd reckon he loved money."

She shook her head, and the thundercloud hair stirred. "Mr. Onselm never needs any money. He takes what he wants, without paying for it."

"Including you?" I asked.

"Not including me yet." She shuddered again. "He reckons to do that later on."

I put down my dime I had left from what Mr. Bristow had gifted me. "Let's have a coke drink together, you and me."

She rang up the dime too. There was a sort of dried-out chuckle at the door, like a stone flung rattling down a deep dark well. I looked quick, and I saw two long, dark wings flop away outside. The Ugly Bird had come to spy what we were doing.

But the girl Winnie hadn't seen, and she smiled over her coke drink. I asked her permission to open my fish and crackers on the bench outside. She said I could. Out there, I worried open the can with that little key that comes with it, and had my meal. When I'd finished I put the empty can and cracker box in a garbage barrel and tuned my guitar.

Hearing that, Winnie came out. She told me how to make my way to the pass and on beyond to Hark Mountain. Of the Bottomless Pool she'd heard some talk, though she'd never been to it. Then she harked while I picked the music and sang the song about the girl whose hair was like the thundercloud before the rain comes down. Harking, Winnie blushed till she was pale no more.

Then we talked about Mr. Onselm and the Ugly Bird, and how they had been seen in two different places at once. "But," said Winnie, "nobody's ever seen the two of them together."

"I have," I told her. "And not an hour back."

And I related about how Mr. Onselm had sat, all sick and miserable, on that rotten log, and how the Ugly Bird had lighted beside him and crowded up to him.

She was quiet to hear all about it, with her eyes staring off, the way she might be looking for something far away. When I was done, she said: "John, you tell me it crowded right up to him."

"It did that thing," I said again. "You'd think it was studying how to crawl right inside him."

"Inside him!"

"That's the true fact."

She kept staring off, and thinking.

"Makes me recollect something I heard somebody say once about hoodoo folks," she said after a time. "How there's hoodoo folks can sometimes put a sort of stuff out, mostly in a dark room. And the stuff is part of them, but it can take the shape and mind of some other person—and once in a while, the shape and mind of an animal."

"Shoo," I said, "now you mention it, I've heard some talk of the same thing. And somebody reckoned it might could explain those Louisiana stories about the werewolves."

"The shape and mind of an animal," she repeated herself. "Maybe the shape and mind of a bird. And that stuff, they call it echo—no, ecto—ecto—"

"Ectoplasm." I remembered the word. "That's it. I've even seen a book with pictures in it, they say were taken of such stuff. And it seems to be alive. It'll yell if you grab it or hit it or stab at it or like that."

"Couldn't maybe—" Winnie began, but a musical voice interrupted.

"I say he's been around here long enough," Mr. Onselm was telling somebody.

Back he came. Behind him were three men. Mr. Bristow was one, and there was likewise a tall, gawky man with wide shoulders and a black-stubbly chin, and behind him a soft, smooth-grizzled old man with an old fancy vest over his white shirt.

Mr. Onselm was like the leader of a posse. "Sam Heaver," he crooned at the soft grizzled one, "do you favor having tramps come and loaf around your store?"

The soft old storekeeper looked at me, dead and gloomy. "You better get going, son," he said, as if he'd memorized it.

I laid my guitar on the bench beside me, very careful of it. "You men ail my stomach," I said, looking at them, from one to the next to the next. "You come at the whistle of this half-born, half-bred witch-man. You let him sic you on me like dogs, when I'm hurting nobody and nothing."

"Better go," said the old storekeeper again.

I stood up and faced Mr. Onselm, ready to fight him. He just laughed at me, like a sweetly played horn.

"You," he said, "without a dime in your pocket! What are you a-feathering up about? You can't do anything to anybody."

Without a dime. . . .

But I'd had a dime. I'd spent it for the coke drinks for Winnie and me. And the Ugly Bird had spied in to see me spend it, my silver money, the silver money that scared and ailed Mr. Onselm. . . .

"Take his guitar, Hobe." Mr. Onselm said an order, and the gawky man moved, clumsy but quickly and grabbed my guitar off the bench and back away to the inner door.

"There," said Mr. Onselm, sort of purring, "that takes care of him."

He fairly jumped, too, and grabbed Winnie by her wrist. He pulled her along out of the porch toward the trail, and I heard her whimper.

"Stop him!" I yelled out, but the three of them stood and looked, scared to move or say a word. Mr. Onselm, still holding Winnie with one hand, faced me. He lifted his other hand and stuck out the pink forefinger at me, like the barrel of a pistol.

Just the look his two eyes, squint and wide, gave me made me weary and dizzy to my bones. He was going to witch me, as he'd done the mules, as he'd done the woman who'd tried to hide her cake from him. I turned away from his gaze, sick and—sure, I was afraid. And I heard him giggle, thinking he'd won already. I took a step, and I was next to that gawky fellow named Hobe, who held my guitar.

I made a quick long jump and started to wrestle it away from him.

"Hang onto that thing, Hobe!" I heard Mr. Onselm sort of choke out, and, from Mr. Bristow:

"Take care, there's the Ugly Bird!"

Its big dark wings flapped like a storm in the air just behind me. But I'd shoved my elbow into Hobe's belly-pit and I'd torn my guitar from his hands, and I turned on my heel to face what was being brought upon me.

A little way off in the open, Mr. Onselm stood stiff and straight as a stone figure in front of an old court house. He still held Winnie by the wrist. Right betwixt them came a-swooping the Ugly Bird at me, the ugliest ugly of all, its long sharp beak pointing for me like a sticky knife.

I dug my toes and smashed my guitar at it. I swung the way a player swings a ball bat at a pitched ball. Full-slam I struck its bulgy head, right above that sharp beak and across its two eyes, and I heard the loud noise as the polished wood of my music-maker crashed to splinters.

Oh, gentlemen, and down went that Ugly Bird!

Down it went, falling just short of the porch.

Quiet it lay.

Its great big feathered wings stretched out either

side, without ary flutter to them. Its beak was driven into the ground like a nail. It didn't kick or flop or stir once.

But Mr. Onselm, where he stood holding Winnie, screamed out the way he might scream if something had clawed out his all insides with one single tearing dig and grab.

He didn't move. I don't even know if his mouth came rightly open to make that scream. Winnie gave a pull with all the strength she had, and tottered back, loose from him. Then, as if only his hold on her had kept him standing, Mr. Onselm slapped right over and dropped down on his face, his arms flung out like the Ugly Bird's wings, his face in the dirt like the Ugly Bird's face.

Still holding onto my broken guitar by the neck, like a club, I walked over to him and stopped. "Get up," I bade him, and took hold of what hair he had and lifted up his face to look at it.

One look was a plenty. From the war, I know a dead man when I see one. I let go Mr. Onselm's hair, and his face went back into the dirt the way you'd know it belonged there.

The other men moved at last, slow and tottery like old men. And they didn't act like my enemies now, for Mr. Onselm who'd made them act thataway was down and dead.

Then Hobe gave a sort of shaky scared shout, and we looked where he was looking.

The Ugly Bird looked all of a sudden rotten and mushy, and while we saw that, it was soaking into the ground. To me, anyhow, its body had seemed to turn shadowy and misty, and I could see through it, to pebbles on the ground beneath. I moved close, though I didn't relish moving. The Ugly Bird was melting away, like dirty snow on top of a hot stove; only no wetness left behind.

It was gone, while we watched and wondered and felt bad all over, and at the same time glad to see it go. Nothing left but the hole punched in the dirt by its beak. I stepped closer yet, and with my shoe I stamped the hole shut.

Then Mr. Bristow kneeled on his knee and turned Mr. Onselm over. On the dead face ran lines across, thin and purple, as though he'd been struck down by a blow from a toaster or a gridiron.

"Why," said Mr. Bristow. "Why, John, them's the marks of your guitar strings." He looked up at me. "Your silver guitar strings."

"Silver?" said the storekeeper. "Is them strings silver? Why, friends, silver finishes a hoodoo man."

That was it. All of us remembered that at once.

"Sure enough," put in Hobe. "Ain't it a silver bullet that it takes to kill a witch, or hanging or burning? And a silver knife to kill a witch's cat?"

"And a silver key locks out ghosts, doesn't it?" said Mr. Bristow, getting up to stand among us again.

I looked at my broken guitar and the dangling strings of silver.

"What was the word you said?" Winnie whispered to me.

"Ectoplasm," I replied her. "Like his soul coming out of him—and getting itself struck dead outside his body."

Then there was talk, more important, about what to do now. The men did the deciding. They allowed to report to the county seat that Mr. Onselm's heart had stopped on him, which was what it had done, after all. They went over the tale three-four times, to make sure they'd all tell it the same. They cheered up while they talked it. You couldn't ever call for a bunch of gladder folks to get shed of a neighbor.

Then they tried to say their thanks to me.

"John," said Mr. Bristow, "we'd all of us sure enough be proud and happy if you'd stay here. You took his curse off us, and we can't never thank you enough."

"Don't thank me," I said. "I was fighting for my life."

Hobe said he wanted me to come live on his farm and help him work it on half shares. Sam Heaver offered me all the money he had in his old cash register. I thanked them. To each I said, no, sir, thank you kindly, I'd better not. If they wanted their tale to sound true to the sheriff and the coroner, they'd better help it along by forgetting that I'd ever been around when Mr. Onselm's heart stopped. Anyhow, I meant to go look at that Bottomless Pool. All I was truly sorry about was my guitar had got broken.

But while I was saying all that, Mr. Bristow had gone running off. Now he came back, with a guitar he'd had at his place, and he said he'd be honored if I'd take it instead of mine. It was a good guitar, had a fine tone. So I put my silver strings on it and tightened and tuned them, and tried a chord or two.

Winnie swore by all that was pure and holy she'd pray for me by name each night of her life, and I told her that that would sure enough see me safe from any assault of the devil.

"Assault of the devil, John!" she said, almost shrill in the voice, she meant it so truly. "It's been you who drove the devil from out this valley."

And the others all said they agreed her on that.

"It was foretold about you in the Bible," said Winnie, her voice soft again. " 'There was a man sent from God, whose name was John—' "

But that was far too much for her to say, and she dropped her sweet dark head down, and I saw her mouth tremble and two tears sneak down her cheeks. And I was that abashed, I said goodbye all around in a hurry.

Off I walked toward where the pass would be, strumming my new guitar as I walked. Back into my mind I got an old, old song. I've heard tell that the song's written down in an old-timey book called *Percy's Frolics,* or *Relics,* or some such name:

"Lady, I never loved witchcraft,
 Never dealt in privy wile,
But evermore held the high way
 Of love and honor, free from guile...."

And though I couldn't bring myself to look back yonder to the place I was leaving forever, I knew that Winnie was a-watching me, and that she listened, listened, still she had to strain her ears to catch the last, faintest end of my song.

WHY THEY'RE NAMED THAT

If the gardinel's an old folks' tale, I'm honest to tell you it's a true one.

Few words about them are best, I should reckon. They look some way like a shed or cabin, snug and rightly made, except the open door might could be a mouth, the two little windows might could be eyes. Never you'll see one on main roads or near towns; only back in the thicketty places, by high trails among tall ridges, and they show themselves there when it rains and storms and a lone farer hopes to come to a house to shelter him.

The few that's lucky enough to have gone into a gardinel and win out again, helped maybe by friends with axes and corn knives to chop in to them, tell that inside it's pinky-walled and dippy-floored, with on the floor all the skulls and bones of those who never did win out; and from the floor and the walls come spouting rivers of wet juice that stings, and as they tell this, why, all at once you know that inside a gardinel is like a stomach.

Down in the lowlands I've seen things grow they name the Venus flytrap and the pitcher plant, that can tole in bugs and flies to eat. It's just a possible chance that the gardinel is some way the same specie, only it's so big it can tole in people.

Gardinel. Why they're named that I can't tell you, so don't inquire me.

ONE OTHER

Up on Hark Mountain I climbed all alone, by a trail as steep as a ladder and no way near as easy to hold to. Under my old army shoes was sometimes mud, sometimes rock, sometimes rolling gravel. I laid hold on laurel and oak scrub and sourwood and dogwood to help me get up the steepest places. Sweat soaked the back of my hickory shirt through and hung under the band of my old hat. Even my silver-strung guitar, bouncing on its sling cord behind me, felt as weighty as an anvil. Hark Mountain's not the highest I ever went up, but it's sure enough one of the steepest.

I reckoned I was getting close to the top when I heard a murmuring voice up there, a young-sounding woman's voice. All at once she yelled out a name, and the name was mine.

"JOHN!" she said, and murmured lower again, and then. "JOHN . . ."

Gentlemen, you can wager I purely sailed up the last stretch of that trail, on my hands and knees, to the very top.

On top of Hark Mountain's tipmost top was a pool.

Hush, gentlemen, without ary stream or draw or branch to feed it, where no pool should ought by nature to be expected, there was a clear blue pool, bright-looking but not just exactly sweet-looking. The highest place on Hark Mountain wasn't any much bigger than a well-sized farmyard, and it had room for hardly the pool and its rim of tight-set rocks. And the trees that grew betwixt those tight rocks at the rim looked leafless and gnarly, but alive. Their branch-twigs crimped and crooked, like claw-nails ready to seize on something.

Almost in reach of me, by the edge of the pool, burnt a fire, and to tend it kneeled down a girl.

She was a tall girl, but not strong built like country girls. She was built slim, like town girls, and she wore town clothes—a white blouse-shirt, and dark pants tight to her long legs all the way up and down, and soft shoes like slippers on her feet. Her arms and neck were as brown as nut meat, the way fashionly women seek to be brown. Around her head was tied a blue silk handkerchief.

Kneeling, she put a tweak of stuff on the fire, and I saw her long, sharp, red fingernails. She spoke again, singing almost, and my name rose out of what she said:

"It is the bones of *John* that I trouble. I for *John* burn this laurel."

On the fire she put some laurel leaves and they sent up steam.

"Even as it crackles and burns, even thus may the flesh of *John* burn for me."

In went something else.

"Even as I melt this wax, with *One Other* to aid me, so speedily may *John* for love of me be melted."

She took up a little clay pot and dripped something. *Drip*, the fire danced. *Drip*, it danced again, jumping up. *Drip*, a third jumpup dancing flame.

"Thrice I pour libation," she said. "Thrice, by *One Other*, I say the spell. Be it with a friend he tarries, with a woman he lingers, may *John* utterly forget and forsake them."

Then she stood up, slim and tall, and held out something red and wavy that I knew.

"This from *John* I took, and now I cast it into—"

But quick and quiet I was close beside her, and I snatched that red scarf away.

"It's been wondering me where I might could have lost that," I said, and she turned and faced me.

Just some slight bit I felt I knew her from somewhere. She was yellow-haired, blue-eyed, brown-faced. She had a little bitty nose, and a mouth as red as red wine. Her blue eyes widened out almost as wide as the blue pool itself, and she smiled. Her teeth were big and white and even in her smile.

"John," she said my name softer, halfway singing it to me. "I was saying the spell for the third time, and you came here to my call." She licked those red lips of hers, and they shone. "Just the way Mr. Howsen promised you'd come."

I never let on to know who Mr. Howsen might possibly be. I wadded up the red scarf into the hip pocket of my blue jeans pants.

"Why were you witch-spelling me?" I inquired her. "What did I ever do to you? I even disremember where it was I met you."

"You don't remember me?" she said, smiling. "But do you remember Enderby Lodge, John?"

"Why, sure."

A month back I'd strolled through those parts with my guitar. Old Major Enderby had bade me rest my hat a while. He was having a dance, and to pleasure him and his guests I'd picked and sung for them.

"You must have been there," I said. "But what was it I did to you?"

Her lips tightened, and now they looked as red and hard and sharp as her painted nails. "Nothing at all, John," she told me. "Not a thing. You did nothing. You ignored me. Doesn't it make you furious to be ignored?"

"Ignored? No, ma'am, it never makes me furious, or I'd be furious a big part of the time."

"It makes me furious. I don't often look at a man twice, and usually they look at me at least once. I don't forgive being ignored." Again she licked her mouth, like a cat over a basin of milk. "I'd been told my charm can be said three times, besides the Bottomless Pool on Hark Mountain, to burn a man's soul with love. And here you came when I called you. Don't shake your head like that, John. You're in love with me."

"I'm sorry, ma'am, I ask your pardon humbly. I'm not in love with you any such thing."

She smiled in pride and scorn, the smile you'd give to a liar. "But you climbed up Hark Mountain to me."

"I reckoned I'd like to have a look at the Bottomless Pool."

"People don't know Bottomless Pool is up here. Only Mr. Howsen and his sort come here. When you talk about bottomless pools, you mean the ones near Lake Lure, on Highway 74."

"Those aren't rightly bottomless," I said. "Anyway, this one, the real one, is sung about in a country song."

Pulling my guitar around. I picked chords and sang:

> "Way up on Hark Mountain
> I climb all alone,
> Where the trail is untravelled,
> The top is unknown.
>
> "Way up on Hark Mountain
> Is the Bottomless Pool.
> You look in its water
> And it shows you a fool."

"You're making that up," she charged me.

"No, ma'am, it was made up long before my daddy's daddy was born. Most country songs have got truth in them. It was the song fetched me here, not your witch-spell."

She laughed, short and sharp, she almost yelped her laugh. "Call it the long arm of coincidence, John. You're here, anyway. Go look in the water and see whether it shows you a fool."

Plainly she didn't know the next verse, so I sang that, too:

> "You can boast of your knowledge
> And brag of your sense,
> It won't make no difference
> A hundred years hence."

Stepping one foot on a rock of the rim, I looked down.

The water didn't show me a fool nor either a wise man. I could see down forever and forever, and I recollected all I'd ever heard tell about the Bottomless Pool. How it was as blue as the blue sky, but it had a special light of its own; how no water ever ran into it, excusing some rain, but it always stayed full; how you couldn't measure its bottom, if you let down a sinker on a line it would go down till the line broke of its own weight.

Though I couldn't spy out the bottom, it wasn't rightly dark down there. Like a man looking up into the blue sky, I looked down into the blue water, and in the blue, far away down, was a many-colored shine, like lights deeper than I could tell you.

"I didn't need to use that stolen scarf," she said at my elbow. "You're lying about why you came here. My spell brought you."

"I'm sorry to say, ma'am," I replied, "I can't even call your name to my mind."

"Do names make a difference if you love me? Call me Annalinda. I'm rich. I've been loved for that alone, and for myself alone."

"Well, I'm plain and poor," I told her. "I was raised hard and put up wet. I don't have ary cent of money in these old clothes of mine. It sure enough wonders me, Miss Annalinda, why you think you need to bother yourself about me."

"I'm just not used to being ignored," she said again.

Down there in the Bottomless Pool's blueness wasn't a fish or a weed of grass. Only that deep-away sparkly flash of lights, changing as you see changes on a bubble of soap blown by a little baby child.

Somebody cleared his throat and said, "I see the spell I gave you worked, ma'am."

I knew Mr. Howsen as he came up the trail to the top of Hark Mountain.

He was purely ugly. I'd been knowing him ten years, and he looked as ugly that minute as the first time I'd seen him, with his mean face and his great big hungry nose and the black patch over one eye. When he'd had his two eyes, they were put so close together in his head you'd be sworn he could look through a keyhole with the two of them at once.

"Yes," said Miss Annalinda. "I want to pay you what I owe you."

"No, ma'am, you pay One Other," said Mr. Howsen, and put his hands in the pockets of the long black coat he wore summer and winter. "For value received, ma'am. I only passed along his word to you."

He tighted his lips at me, in what wasn't anything like a smile. "John," he said, "you relish journeying. You've relished it ever since you was just a chap, going what way you felt like going. You've seen a right much of this world. But she toled you to her, and now you'll stay with her, and for that you can be obliged to One Other."

"One other what?" I inquired him.

Though that was just a defy at him. Of course, a-hearing of Hark Mountain and the Bottomless Pool, I'd sure enough heard of One Other. How mountain folks swear he's got the one arm and the one leg only, that he runs fast on the one leg and grabs hold with the one arm, and whatever he grabs goes with him into the Bottomless Pool. And that it's One Other's power and knowledge that lets witches do their spells up there by the Bottomless Pool.

"Be here with the lady when One Other asks payment," said Mr. Howsen. "That there spell was good a many years before Theocritus written it down in old Greek. It'll still be good when English writing is as old as Greek writing. It toled you here."

But for the life of me I couldn't recollect seeing Miss Annalinda at Major Enderby's. "My own wish and will brought me here, not hers," I said. "I wanted to see the Bottomless Pool. I wonder at that soap-bubble color in it."

"Ain't any soap in there, John," said Mr. Howsen. "Soap bubbles don't never get so big as to have all that much color."

"You rightly sure about how big soap bubbles get, Mr. Howsen?" I asked. "Once I heard a science doctor say how this whole life of ours, the heaven and the earth, the sun and moon and stars and all, may be holding a shape like a big soap bubble. He said it stretched and spread like a soap bubble, with all the suns and stars and worlds getting farther off apart as time passes."

"Both of you stay here where you are," Mr. Howsen bade us. "One Other's going to want to find the both of you here."

"But—" Miss Annalinda made out to begin.

"Both of you stay," Mr. Howsen said again, and with his shoe toe he scuffed a mark across the head of the trail. Then he hawked, and spit on the mark. "Don't cross that line. It would be worse for you than if fire burnt you behind and before, inside and out."

Like a lizard he bobbed over the edge and away down the trail.

"Let's us go too," I said to Miss Annalinda, but she stared at the mark made by Mr. Howsen's shoe, and the healthy blood had paled out from under the tan on her face.

"Pay him no mind," I said. "Let's start, it's coming on to sunset."

"He said not to cross the mark," she reminded me, scared.

"I don't care a shuck for aught he said. Come on, Miss Annalinda," and I took her by the arm.

That quick I had her to fight. Holding to her arm was like holding the spoke of a runaway wheel. Her other hand came up and her sharp red nails racked hide and blood off my cheek, and she tried to bite. I couldn't hold her without hitting her, so I turned her loose, and she sat down on a rock by the poolside and cried into her hands.

"Then I'll have to go alone," I said, and took a step.

"John!" she called, loud and shaky as a horse's whinny. "If you step across that mark, I'll throw myself into this Bottomless Pool!"

Sometimes you can tell when a woman means the thing she says. This was one of the times. So I walked back to her, and she was a-looking to where the downsinking sun made the edge of the sky turn red and fiery. It would be cold and dark when that sun was gone. With trembling hands she smoothed the tight pants tighter to her legs.

"I'll just build up the fire," I said, and tried to break off a branch from a claw-looking tree.

But it was tough and had thorny stickers. So I went to the edge of the open place, off from where Mr. Howsen had drawn his mark on us, and gathered up an armful of deadfallen wood. I brought it back and freshened the fire she'd made for her witching. It blazed up red, the color of the sun that sank down. High in the sky, that turned pale before it would turn dark, slid a great big old buzzard. Its wings flopped, slow and heavy, spreading out their feathers like long fingers.

"You don't believe all this, John," said Miss Annalinda, in a voice that sounded as if she was just before freezing from the cold. "But the spell was true. The rest of it's true, too, about One Other. He must have been here since the beginning of time."

"No, that's one thing peculiar enough to be the truth," I answered her. "There's not much been told about One Other till this last year or so. About his being here at the Bottomless Pool, or about folks being able to do witch things with his help, or how he aids the witches and takes payment for his aid. It's no old country tale, it's right new and recent."

"Payment," she said after me. "What kind of payment?"

I poked up the fire. "That all depends. Sometimes one thing, sometimes another. You notice how Mr. Howsen goes around with only the one eye. I've heard it said that One Other took an eye from him. Maybe he won't want an eye from you, but he'll want something. Something for nothing."

"What do you mean?" and she frowned her brows at me.

"You put a witch-spell on me to make me love you, but you don't love me. You did it for spite, not love."

"Why—why—"

Nothing devils a woman like being caught in the truth. She laid hold on a poolside rock next to her.

"That will smash my head or either my guitar," I gave her quick word. "Smash my head, and you're up here on the mountain, all alone with a dead corpse. Smash my guitar, and I'll go right down the trail."

"And I'll jump in the pool."

"All right, you can jump. I won't stay where folks fling rocks at me. Fair warning's as good as a promise."

She let go the rock again. She was ready to start crying. I came and set my foot at the edge of the pool and looked down into the water.

By now the sky was a-getting purely dark, but low down and away down was that soap-bubble shiny light. I brought back to mind an old old tale they say came from the Indians who owned the mountains back before the first white folks came. It was about people living above the sky and thinking their world was the only one, till somebody pulled up a great long root, and through the hole they could see down to another world below, where people lived. Then Miss Annalinda began to talk.

She was talking for the company of her own voice, and she talked about herself. About her rich father and her rich mother, and all her rich aunts and uncles and rich friends, the money and automobiles and land and horses they owned, and the big chance of men who wanted to marry her. One was the son of folks as rich as her folks. One was the governnor of the state, who was ready to put away his wife if Miss Annalinda said the word she'd have him. And one was a nobleborn man from a foreign country.

"And you'd marry me too, John," she said.

"I'm just sorry to death," I said. "But I shouldn't."

"Now you're lying, John."

"I never lie, Miss Annalinda."

"Everybody lies. Well, talk to me, anyway. This isn't any sort of place to keep quiet in."

So I talked in my turn, about myself. How I'd been born next to Drowning Creek and baptized in its waters. How my folks had died in two days of each other, how an old teacher lady had taught me to read and write, and I'd taught myself how to play the guitar. How I'd roamed and rambled. How I'd fought in the war, and a thousand had fallen at my side and ten thousand at my right hand, but it hadn't come nigh me. I left out some things, like meeting up with the Ugly Bird, because she was nervous enough. I said that though I'd never had aught and never rightly expected to have aught, yet I'd always made out for bread to eat and sometimes butter on it.

"How about pretty girls, John?" she asked me. "You must have had regiments of them."

"None to mention," I said, for it wouldn't have

been proper to mention them. "Miss Annalinda, it's a-getting full dark."

"And the moon's up."

"No, ma'am, that's the soap-bubble light from down there in the Bottomless Pool."

"You make me shiver!" she scolded at me, and drew up her shoulders. "What do you mean with all this talk about soap bubbles?"

"Only just what I was telling Mr. Howsen. That science man said our whole life, what he called our universe, was swelling and stretching out, so that suns and moons and stars pull farther apart all the time. He said our world and all the other worlds are inside that stretching skin of suds that makes the bubble. We can't study out what's outside the bubble, or either inside, only just what's in the suds part. It sounds crazyish but when he talked it sounded true."

"That's not a new idea, John. James Jeans wrote a book about it, *The Expanding Universe*. But where does the soap bubble come from?"

"I reckon that Whoever made all things must have blown it, from a bubble pipe too big for us to study out."

She snickered, so she must have been feeling better. "You believe in a God who blows soap bubbles." Then she didn't snicker. "How long do we have to go on waiting here?"

"No time at all. We can go whenever you're ready."

"No," she said, "we have to stay."

"Then we'll stay till One Other come. He'll come. Mr. Howsen's a despicable man, but he knows about One Other."

"Oh!" she cried out. "I only wish he'd come and get it over with."

And her wish came true.

The firelight had risen high, and as she spoke something hiked up behind the rocks on the pool's edge. It hiked up like a wet black leech, but much bigger by about a thousand times. It slid and oozed to the top of a rock, and as it waited a second, wet and shiny in the firelight, it looked as if somebody had flung down a wet coat. Then it hunched and swelled, and its edges came apart.

It was a wet hand, as broad in the back as a shovel, and with fingers as long as the tines of a hayfork.

"Get up and start down trail," I said to Miss Annalinda as quiet and calm as I could make out to be. "Don't argue, just start."

"Why should I?" she snapped out, without moving, and by then she saw, too, and any chance for her to get away was gone.

The hayfork fingers grabbed hold of the rock, and a head and shoulder heaved up to where we could see them.

The shoulder was like a cypress root humping out of the water, and the head was like a dark pumpkin, round and smooth and bald, with no face, only two eyes. They were green, but not bright green like cat-eyes or dog-eyes in the night. They were stale rotten green, like something spoiled.

Miss Annalinda's shriek was like a train blowing for a crossing. She jumped up, but she didn't run. Maybe she couldn't. Then a big black knee lifted into sight, and all of One Other came up out of the Bottomless Pool and rose straight up before us.

One Other was twice as tall as a tall man, and it was sure enough true that he had just the one arm and the one leg. The arm would be his left arm, and the leg his right leg. Maybe that's why the mountain folks had named him One Other. But his stale green eyes were two and both of them looked down at us. He made a sure hop on his big single foot, big and flat as the top of a table, and he put out his hand to touch or to grab.

I dragged Miss Annalinda clear back around the fire. I reckon she'd fainted, or near to. Her feet didn't work under her, she only moaned, and she was double heavy in my arms, the way a limp weight can be. My strength was under tax to pull her toward where I'd flung down my guitar. I wanted to get my hands on the guitar. It might could be a weapon—its music or its silver strings might be a distaste to an unchancey thing like One Other.

But One Other had circled the fire the other way around, so that we came almost in touch again. He stood on his one big foot, between me and my guitar. It might be ill or well to him, but I couldn't get it and find out.

Even then, the thought of running across Mr. Howsen's mark and down the mountain in the night never entered my head. I stood still, holding Miss Annalinda on her feet that were gone so limp her shoes were near about to drop off, and looked up twice my height into what wasn't a face save for those two green eyes.

"What have you got in mind!" I inquired One Other, as if he could understand my talk; and the words, almost in Miss Annalinda's ear, brought back her strength and wits. She stood alone still shoving herself close against me. She looked up at One Other, and she said a couple of holy names.

One Other bent his big lumpy knee and sank his bladdery dark body down and put out that big splay paw of his. The firelight showed his open palm, slate gray, and things dribbling out from it in a clinking, jangling little strew at our feet. He straightened up again.

"Oh, John!" And Miss Annalinda dropped down to grab. "Look, he's giving us—"

Tugging my eyes away from One Other's, I looked at what she held out to me. It shone and lighted up, like a hailstone by lantern light. It was the size of a hen egg, and it had a many little edges and flat faces, all full of fire, pale and blue outside and innerly many-colored like the soap-bubble light in the Bottomless Pool. She shoved it into my hand, and it felt slippery and sticky, like soap. I flung it on the ground again.

"You fool, that's a diamond!" she squeaked at me. "It's bigger than the Orloff, bigger than the Koh-i-noor!"

She scrabbled with both hands for more of the shiny things, that lighted up with every color you could call for. "Here's an emerald," she yipped, "and here's a ruby. John he's our friend, he's giving us things worth more money than—"

Down on her knees before One Other, she clawed up two fistfuls of those things he'd flung for her to get down and gather. But I had my eyes back on him. He was looking at me—not at her, he was sure of her. Well he knew humankind's greed for shiny stones. About me, he wasn't sure yet. He studied me as I've seen folks to study an animal, to see whether to hit it with a stick or slice it with a knife. The shiny stones didn't fetch me. He reckoned to find something that would.

Oh, I know how like a crazy tale to scare young ones all this sounds. But there and then, One Other was so plain to see and make out, the way you could see him if I was to make a clay image of him and stand it up on one leg in your sight, and it grew till it was twice as tall as you, with stale green eyes and one hayfork paw and one table-top foot. In a moment there, with no sound, he and I looked at one another. Miss Annalinda, down on the ground between us, gopped and goggled at the stones she scooped up in her hands. Then the silence broke. A drop of water fell. Another. *Drip, drip, drip,* like what Miss Annalinda had dripped into the fire—water from the Bottomless Pool, dripping off of One Other's body and head and his one arm and his one leg.

Then he turned his eyes and mind back to Miss Annalinda, for long enough to spare me for a big jump past him to where my guitar was.

He turned quick and swung down at me with his

paw, like a man swatting a bug; but I had the guitar and I was running backward out of his reach. I got the guitar across me, my left hand on the frets, and my right hand a-clawing the silver strings. They sang out, and One Other teetered on the broad sole of that foot, cocked his head to hark.

I started the *Last Judgment Song*, the one old Uncle T. P. Hinnard had told me long ago was good against evil things:

> "Three holy kings, four holy saints,
> At heaven's high gate that stand,
> Speak out to bid all evil wait
> And stir no foot or hand. . . ."

But he came at me anyway. The charm wasn't serving against One Other, as I'd been vowed to it would serve against any evil in this world. One Other wasn't of this world, though just now he was in it. He was from the Bottomless Pool, and from whatever was beyond, below, behind where its bottom had ought to be.

I ran around the fire and around Miss Annalinda still crouched down among all those jewels. After me he hopped, like the almightiest big one-legged rabbit in song or tale. He had me almost headed off, coming alongside me, and I ran right through the fire that was less fear to me than he was. My shoes kicked its coals as I ran through. On the far side I made myself stop and turn again. Because I had to face him somehow. I couldn't just run off from him and leave Miss Annalinda to pay, all alone, for her foolishness.

He'd stopped, too, in his one track. The fire, scattered by my feet, blazed up in scattered chunks, and he was sort of pulling himself together and back from it. *Drip, drip*, the water fell off him. I felt there couldn't be any standing that dripping noise, so I sang out loud with another verse of the *Last Judgment Song:*

"The fire from heaven will fall at last
On wealth and pride and power—
We will not know the minute, and
We will not know the hour. . . ."

One Other hopped a long hop back, away from the fire and away from me and away from the song.

Something whispered me what I'd needed to know.

From out the water he'd come. If I didn't want him to get me, to hold me at a price I'd never redeem—the way jewels beyond all reckoning could buy Miss Annalinda—I'd have to fight him like any water thing.

Fight fire with water, wise folks say. Fire and water are sworn enemies. Fight water with fire. . . .

He circled around again, and that time I didn't flee from before him. I grabbed down toward the scattering of the fire. One Other's big flat hand slapped me spinning away, but my own hand had snatched up a burning chunk. When I staggered back onto my feet, I still held my guitar in one fist, the chunk in the other.

I whipped that fire in a whirl around my head, and it blazed up like pure lightwood. As One Other came bending down for me again, I rushed to meet him and I shoved the fire at him.

He couldnt face it. He broke back from it. I jumped sidewise my own self, so that he was between me and the fire, and sashayed that burning stick at him again. He jumped back, and his foot slammed right down among the coals.

Gentlemen, I hope none of you all ever hear such a sound as he made, with no mouth to make it. Not a yell or a roar or a scream, but the whole top of Hark Mountain hummed and danced to it. He flung himself clear of the fire again, hurting and shaking every ounce of him, and then I stabbed my torch like a spear for where his face ought to be, and made a direct hit.

I tell you, he couldn't front up to fire, he couldn't

stand it. He just spun around and jumped, and then he dived into the water from which he'd come to us, into the Bottomless Pool, and the splash he made was like a wagon falling from a bridge. Running to the rocks, I saw him cleave down below there, into the deep clearness, like a diving one-legged frog—all among the soap-bubble colors, getting small while I watched, so small he looked a hand's size. A finger's size. A bean's size. And then the light gulped him. And he was gone from my sight.

I stepped back to the scattered fire, and dropped my burning chunk.

Miss Annalinda still huddled on the ground. I question whether she'd paid aught of mind to what had gone on, that scrambling fight. Her hands were grabbed full of jewels shining green, red, blue, white, all colors.

I said nothing, but took her by the arm and pulled her to her feet. She looked at me and waved her both full fists in joy.

"Give them here," I said.

Her eyes stabbed at me like fish gigs. She couldn't believe I'd spoken such words. I put down my guitar and took her right wrist and pried open her right hand. I tried not to hurt her as I took the jewels. Into the Bottomless Pool I plunged them, one by one. They splashed and sank down like pebbles.

"Don't, John!" she screamed, but I took her other hand and pried away the rest of them. *Plop,* I flung one after the first bunch. *Plop,* I flung another. *Plop, plop, plop,* more.

"They're a fortune," she gabbled, dragging at my arm. "The greatest fortune ever dreamed of—"

"No, ma'am," I said. "A misfortune. The greatest misfortune ever dreamed of."

"But no!"

Plop, plop, I flung them in, the last of the jewels. "What were you ready to pay for them?" I inquired her.

"Anything," she said as if she was tired out. "Anything."

"You mean everything. If he paid high for us, he meant to have his worth from us. He needs folks of this world to serve him, more folks than just Mr. Howsen." I pointed into the Bottomless Pool, for her to look down there. "I hope and pray he stays now, where things are more comfortable than what taste I gave him."

She looked, down to where the Bottomless Pool had no bottom.

"John, you're right," she said, as if she talked out of a dream. "Those colors do look like the tints of a soap bubble—stretched out, with nothing beyond its film of suds that we can imagine. A great big unthinkable soap bubble, like the one you say God blew."

"Might could be so," I said. "Might could be there's more than the one soap bubble we're in. A right many soap bubbles. Each one a life and a universe strange to this one we're in."

The pain of that new thought went into her like a knife and made her silent. I talked on:

"Might could be there's two soap bubbles touching. And the spot where they come together is where something can leave the one and come into the other."

She sat down. The new thought was weight as well as pain. "Oh," she moaned in herself.

"Some born venturer dares try to move into the new bubble," I said, "through whatever matches the Bottomless Pool on that far side, in that other life and universe. Maybe. I say. There's God's great plenty of maybes about it."

"No maybes," she said, all of a sudden. "You saw him, no such creature was ever born into our world. Anything looking like that must be—"

"You still don't understand," and I shook my head. "I don't truly reckon he'd look like that in his own soap bubble. He makes himself look that way, to be as possibly much like our kind he meets in our world. We can't guess what he'd naturally look like."

"I don't want to guess," and she sounded near about to cry.

"Such a stranger needs friends and helpers in the strange new world. Some things he knows from his own home are like power here, power we think is witch stuff. He'll pay high for helpers like Mr. Howsen. He'd have paid high for us."

"Will he come back?" she asked.

"Not right off." I picked up my guitar. "Let's grope down trail in the dark, so if he does come back he won't find us. Somewhere below we'll build a fire and in the morning get all the way down."

"John," said Miss Annalinda, talking fast, "you were right about me. My spell was to get you up here for spite. But now, if you don't have anywhere to go—"

"I've got everywhere to go," I said. "Soon as I get you down safe, I'll go everywhere."

"It's not spite any more, John, it's love." She said that word as if she'd never said it before. "It's love, I love you, John."

She maybe didn't know that she was lying, and I wanted to stop her.

"You know," I changed the subject, "there's one more thing about this soap-bubble idea. The bubble we live in keeps on a-stretching and a-swelling. But a soap bubble can't last forever. Some time or other, it stretches and swells so tight, it just bursts."

That did what I was after, it stopped her flood of words. She started up and off and all around. I saw the whites of her eyes glitter in the last glow of the fire.

"Bursts?" she said slowly. "Then what?"

"Then nothing. When a soap bubble bursts, it's gone."

And we had silence to start our climb down Hark Mountain.

THEN I WASN'T ALONE

eckoning I had that woodsy place all to myself, I began to pick Pretty Saro on my guitar's silver strings for company. But then I wasn't alone; for soft fluty music began to play along with me.

Looking up sharp, I saw him through the green laurels right in front. He was young. He hadn't a shirt on. Nary razor had touched his soft yellowy young beard. To his mouth he held a sort of hollowed-out twig and his slim fingers danced on and off a line of holes to make the notes. Playing, he smiled at me.

I smiled back, and started The Ring That Has No End. Right away quick he was a-playing that with me, too, soft and sweet and high but not shrill.

He wants to be friends, I told myself, and got up and held my hand out to him.

He whirled around and ran. Just for a second before he was gone, I saw that he was a man only to his waist. Below that he had the legs of a horse, four of them.

SHIVER IN THE PINES

We sat along the edge of Mr. Hoje Cowand's porch, up the high hills of the Rebel Creek country. Mr. Hoje himself, and his neighbor Mr. Eddy Herron who was a widow-man like Mr. Hoje, and Mr. Eddy's son Clay who was a long tall fellow like his daddy, and Mr. Hoje's pretty-cheeked daughter Sarah Ann, who was courting with Clay those days. Those folks, and me. I'd stopped off to hand-help Mr. Hoje to build him a new pole fence, on my way off to Flornoy College to sing to them there. But nothing would do Mr. Hoje but that I'd stay two-three days, till Clay and Sarah Ann's wedding. Supper had been pork and fried apples and pone and snap beans. The sun made to set, and they all asked me to sing.

So I picked the silver strings on my guitar and began with an old tuneful one:

"Choose your partner as you go,
Choose your partner as you go...."

"Yippeehoo!" hollered old Mr. Eddy. "You sure enough chose out of my favorite best, John. Come on, young folks, choose partners and dance!"

Up hopped Clay and Sarah Ann, where the front yard was stomped hard and level, and I played it up loud and sang, and Mr. Eddy called the figures for them to step to:

"Honor your partner! ... Swing your partner! ...

Do-si-do! . . . Allemand right!" Till I got to one last chorus, singing it out for all I could:

> "Fare thee well, my charming girl,
> Fare thee well, I'm gone!
> Fare thee well, my charming girl,
> With golden slippers on!"

"Kiss your partner and turn loose of her!" hollered out Mr. Eddy as I stopped. And Clay kissed Sarah Ann the way you'd think it was his whole business in life, and Sarah Ann, rising up on her little toes, kissed him back.

Mr. Hoje picked up the jug that had his make of whiskey in it, and there never was government whiskey as good as what Mr. Hoje knows to make for his own drinking and his friends'. "Won't be singing and dancing to touch that on the day these young ones marry up," he said, passing the jug to me. "And no fare the wells, neither."

"And I purely wish I could buy you golden slippers, Sarah Ann," said Clay as they sat down together.

"Gold's where you find it," quoted Mr. Eddy from the Bible, and took a whet out of the jug in his turn. "Clay, you might could ransack round them old lost mines the Ancients dug, that nobody knows much about. Remember the song about them, John?"

I remembered it, for Mr. Eddy and Mr. Hoje talked a right much about the Ancients and their mines. I sang it:

> "Where were they, where were they,
>   On that gone and vanished day
> When they shoveled for their treasure of gold?
>   In the pines, in the pines,
>   Where the sun never shines,
> And I shiver when the wind blows cold. . . ."

As I stopped, a fellow coughed. "Odd," said the fellow, walking into the yard, "to hear that song just now."

We didn't know him. He was blocky-made, not young nor either old, with a store suit and a black hat, like a man running for superior court judge. His square face looked flat and white, like a face drawn on paper.

"Might I sit for a minute?" he asked, mannerly. "I've come a long, long way."

"Take a place on this door-log, and welcome," Mr. Hoje invited him. "My name's Hoje Cowand, and this here is my girl Sarah Ann, and these is the Herrons, and this here's John who's a-visiting with me. Come a long way, you said? Where from sir?"

"From going to and fro in the world," said the stranger, lifting the black hat from his smoky-gray hair, "and from walking up and down in it."

That was another quotation from the Bible, and if you've read the first chapter of the Book of Job, you'll know who's supposed to have said it. The man saw how we gopped, for he smiled as he sat down and stuck out his dusty shoes.

"My name's Reed Barnitt," he told us. "Odd, to hear talk of the Ancients and their mines. Because I've been roving around to hear talk about them."

"Why," said Mr. Hoje, "the tale goes that the Ancients come into these here mountains back before the settlers. Close on to four hundred years back."

"That long, Mr. Hoje?" asked young Clay.

"Well, now," Mr. Hoje allowed, "there was a tree cut that had growed up in the mouth of a mine of the Ancients, near Horse Stomp. And there was schooled folks that counted the rings in the wood, and there was full three hundred. It was before the Yankee war they done that counting, so that tree seeded itself in the mine-hole about four hundred years back, or maybe more than that."

"The times of the Spaniards," nodded Reed Barnitt. "Maybe about when Hernando de Soto and his Spanish soldiers came across these mountains."

"I've always heard tell the Ancients was living here around that time," put in Mr. Eddy, "but I've likewise heard tell they wasn't no Spanish folks, nor neither Indians."

"Did they get what they were after?" wondered Reed Barnitt.

"My old daddy went into that Horse Stomp heading once," said Mr. Eddy. "He said it run back about seven hundred feet as he stepped it, and at the end a deep shaft went down. Well, he reckoned no mortal soul would ever dig so far, excusing he found what he was after." He pushed Mr. Hoje's jug toward Reed Barnitt. "Have a dram?"

"Thank you kindly, I don't use it. But what did the Ancients want?"

"Only mine of theirs I seen is over the ridge yonder." Mr. Hoje nodded through the dusk. "Where they call it Black Pine Hollow."

"Where the sun never shines," put in Reed Barnitt, smiling tight at me, "and I shiver when the wind blows cold."

"I was there three-four times when I was a chap," said Mr. Hoje, "but not lately. Folks allows there's hants there. I seen a right much quartz laying round, and I hear tell gold comes from quartz rock."

"Gold," nodded Reed Barnitt, his hand inside his coat. "You folks are treating me clever and friendly, and I hope you'll let me make a gift. Miss Sarah Ann, I myself don't have use for these, so if you'd accept—"

What he held out was golden slippers, that shone in the sun's last bit of light.

Gentlemen, you should have heard Sarah Ann cry out her pleasure, you should have seen the gold shine in her eyes. But she drew back the hand she put out.

"It wouldn't be fitting for me to take them," she said.

"Then I'll just give them to this young man," and Reed Barnitt set the slippers in Clay's lap. "Young sir, I misdoubt if Miss Sarah Ann would refuse a gift at your hands."

The slippers had slim high heels and pointy toes, and they shone like glory. Clay smiled to Sarah Ann and held them out. To see her smile back, you'd think it was Clay and not Reed Barnitt who had taken them from nowhere for her.

"I do thank you kindly," said Sarah Ann. She shucked off scuffy old shoes and the golden slippers fitted her like slippers made to the measure of her little feet. "John," she said "you were just singing about things like this."

"Heard him as I came up trail from Rebel Creek," said Reed Barnitt. "And likewise I heard him sing of the Ancients in Black Pine Hollow." His square face looked at us around. "Gentlemen, I wonder if there's heart in you all to go there with me."

We gopped again. Finally Clay asked, "For gold?"

"For what else?" said Reed Barnitt. "Nobody's found it there, because nobody had the right way of looking for it."

Nary one of us was really surprised to hear what the man said. There'd been such a story as long as anybody had lived around Rebel Creek. Mr. Hoje drank from the jug, and said, "In what respect a special way, Mr. Barnitt?"

"I said, I've roved a far piece. I went to fetch a spell that would show the treasure. But I can't do it alone." Again the white face traveled its look over us. "It takes five folks—men, because a woman mustn't go into a mine."

We knew about that. If lady-folks go down a mine there'll be a miner killed or something else bad to befall.

"You've treated me friendly," said Reed Barnitt again. "I feel like asking you, will you all come help me? Mr. Cowand and Mr. Herron, and you his son, and you, John. Five we'd seek the treasure of the Ancients, and five ways we'd divide it."

Sarah Ann had her manners with her. "I'll go do the dishes," she said to us. "No, Clay, stay and talk here."

Reed Barnitt watched her walk into the house. She left the door open, and the shine from the hearth gave us a red light out there after sundown.

"You're a lucky young rooster," Reed Barnitt said to Clay. "A fifth chunk of the Ancients' treasure would sure enough be a blessing to that girl."

"Mr. Barnitt, I'm with you," Clay quick told him.

"So am I," said Mr. Eddy, because his son had spoken.

"I don't lag back when others say go forward," I added on.

"And count on me," finished Mr. Hoje for us. "That makes five, like what you want it, sir. But you studied the matter out and got the spell. You should ought to have more than a fifth of whatever we find."

But the square white face shook sideways. "No. Part of the spell is that each of the five takes his equal part, of the doing and of the sharing. That's how it must be to come true. Now, we begin."

"This instant?" asked Clay.

"Nary better time than now," said Reed Barnitt. "Stand round, you all."

He got up from the door-log and stepped into the yard, and the three of us with him. "The first part of the spell," he said. "To learn if the Ancients truly left a treasure."

Where the hearth's red glimmer came out on the ground in front of the door, he bent down. He picked up a stick and marked in the dirt.

"Five-pointed star," he said. It was maybe four feet across. "Stand at the points, friends. Yes, like that."

Rising, he stood at the fifth point. He dropped the stick and put a white hand into the side pocket of his coat. "Silence," he bade us, though he didn't need to.

He stooped again and flung something down at the star's center. Maybe it was a handful of powder, though I'm not sure, for it broke out into fire quick, and shone like pure white heat yanked in a chunk from the heart of a furnace. It shone on the gray beards of Mr. Hoje and Mr. Eddy. Clay's young jaws and cheeks looked dull and drawn. Reed Barnitt needed no special light to be pale.

He began to speak: "Moloch, Lucifer," he said in a voice like praying. "Anector, Somiator, sleep ye not, awake. The strong hero Holoba, the powerful Ischiros, the mighty Manus Erohye—show us the truth, Amen!"

Again his hand in his pocket, to bring out a slip of paper the size of a postcard and whiter than the white of the glow. He handed it to Clay who was nearest to him. "Breathe on it," said Reed Barnitt, "and the others do likewise."

Clay breathed on it and passed it to Mr. Hoje. Then it came to me, and to Mr. Eddy, and back to Reed Barnitt. He held it low above that sick-white heat. Back he jumped, quick, and yelled out: "Earth on the fire! Smother it before we lose the true word!"

Clay and his father kicked on dirt. Mr. Hoje and Reed Barnitt walked side by side to the porch, whispering together. Then Mr. Hoje called in to Sarah Ann, "Fetch out the lamp, honey."

She did so. We gathered around to look at the paper. Writing was on it, spidery and rough, the way you'd think it was written in mud instead of ink. Reed Barnitt gave it to Sarah Ann.

"Your heart's pure," he said. "Read out what it says."

She held the lamp in one hand, the paper in the other. " 'Do right, and prosper,' " she read, soft and shaky, " 'and what you seek is yours. Great treasure. Obey orders. To open the way, burn the light—' "

"We've put out the light," said Clay, but Reed Barnitt waved him quiet.

"Turn the paper over, Miss Sarah Ann," said Reed

Barnitt. "Looks to be more to read on the other side."

She went on, from more muddy-looking scrawl on the back:

"'Aram Harnam has the light. Buy it from him, but don't tell him why. He is wicked. Pay what he asks. The power is dear and scarce.'"

She looked up. "That's all it says," she told us, and gave the paper back to Reed Barnitt.

We all sat down, the lamp on the porch floor. "Anybody know that man, what's-his-name?" asked Reed Barnitt.

"We know Aram Harnam," answered Mr. Hoje.

What folks along Rebel Creek said about Aram Harnam wasn't good. Once he went to a college to study to be a preacher, and that college gave him a trial, preaching a sermon to some folks in another county. His teachers went to hear. When he'd done, as I've heard it told, those teachers told Aram Harnam that from what he'd said under pretense of a sermon they wanted him to pack his things and leave that college before another sun rose.

"I take it Aram Harnam's a bad man," Reed Barnitt suggested.

"You take it right, sir," allowed Mr. Eddy. "So does whoever wrote on that there paper."

"Wrote on the paper?" Reed Barnitt repeated him, and held it to the light. It was white and empty; so was the other side when he turned that up.

"The writing's vanished," he said, nodding his pale face above it. "But we all remember what it said. We must buy the light, and not let Aram Harnam know why we want it."

"When do we go see him?" asked Mr. Hoje.

"Why not right now?" said Reed Barnitt, but Mr. Hoje and Mr. Eddy spoke against that. Neither one of them wanted to be a-trucking around Aram Harnam's place in the dark of night. We made it up we'd meet tomorrow morning for breakfast at Mr. Eddy's, and then go.

Mr. Eddy and Clay left. Mr. Hoje and Sarah Ann made up pallets for Reed Barnitt and me just inside the front door. Reed Barnitt slept right off quick, but I lay awake a good spell of time. There was a sight of hoot owls a-hooting in the trees round about the cabin, and a sight of thoughts in my head.

The way I've told it so far, you might could wonder why we came in so quick on Reed Barnitt's spell and scheme. Lying there, I wondered the same thing. It came to mind that Clay had first said he'd join. That was for Sarah Ann, and the hope to make her happy. After Clay spoke, Mr. Eddy and Mr. Hoje felt bound to do the same, for with them the kingdom and the power and the glory tied up to their young ones, and they wanted to see them wed and happy. Mr. Hoje in special. He worked hard on his little place, with corn patches on terraces up slope where you hung on with one hand while you chopped weeds with the other, and just one cow and two hogs in his pens.

I reckoned that hope, more than belief, caused them to say yes to Reed Barnitt. As for me, I'd gone a many miles and seen a right much more than any of my friends, and some of the things not what you'd call everyday things. I hoped for a good piece of luck for Clay and Sarah Ann. Never having had aught myself, or expecting to or needing to, I anyhow saw he and she wanted something. And maybe, with one or two things I'd watched happen, I could know to help out more than either of their fathers.

Figuring thataway, I slept at last, and we all got up soon in the morning to meet at Mr. Eddy's and go to Aram Harnam's.

Seeing Aram Harnam, sitting in front of his squatty-built little cabin, I reckoned I'd never seen a hairier man, and mighty few hairier creatures. He had a juniper-bark basket betwixt his patched knees, and he was picking over a mess of narrow-leafed plants in it. His hands crawled in the basket like black furry spiders. Out betwixt his shaggy black hair and his shaggy black beard looked only his bright eyes and his thin nose, and if he smiled or frowned at us, none could say. He spoke up with a boom, and I recollected how once he'd studied to be a preacher.

"Hoje Cowand," he said, "you're welcome and your friends, too. I knowed youins was coming."

"Who done told you that?" asked Mr. Hoje.

"Little bird done told me," said Aram Harnam. "Little black bird with green eyes, that tells me a many things."

That minded me of the Ugly Bird that once I'd killed to free a whole valley of folks from the scare of it.

"Did your little bird tell you what we want?" asked Mr. Eddy, but Aram Harnam shook his hairy head.

"No, sir, never said what." He put down the basket. "So I'm a-waiting to hear what."

"We want a light of you, Aram Harnam," said Mr. Hoje then. "A special kind of light."

"The light that shows you what you'd miss else?" Aram Harnam leant back against his cabin-logs. "I can fix you such a light."

"How much?" asked Clay.

Aram Harnam's furry hand fiddled in his black beard. "It's a scare thing, that light. Cost you five hundred dollars."

"Five hundred dollars!" howled out Mr. Eddy.

The eyes among Aram Harnam's hair came to me. "Hear that echo, son?" he asked. "These here hills and mountains sure enough give you back echoes. Yes, sir, Mr. Eddy, five hundred dollars."

Mr. Hoje gulped. "We ain't got no such kind of money."

"Got to have that kind of money to buy that kind of light," said Aram Harnam.

"Step aside with me, friends," said Reed Barnitt, and Aram Harnam sat and watched us pull a dozen or twenty steps back to talk with our heads together.

"He guesses something," Reed Barnitt whispered, "but not everything, or I judge he'd put his price higher still. Anyway, our spell last night said there's treasure and we need the light to find it."

"I ain't got but forty dollars," said Mr. Eddy. "Any of youins got enough to put with my forty to make five hundred?"

"Twenty's all I've got," Reed Barnitt said, and breathed long and worried. "That's sixty so far. John?"

"The change in my pockets maybe comes to a dollar," I said. "I'm not certain sure."

Aram Harnam laughed or coughed, once. "Youins sure enough make a big thing out of five hundred dollars," he called to us.

Mr. Hoje faced around. "We don't have that much cash."

"I might could credit you, Hoje Cowand."

"Five hundred dollars' worth?" asked Mr. Hoje. "What on?"

"We-ell," the word came slow out of the hair and whiskers. "You got a piece of land, and a cow and a pig or two."

"I can't give you them," Mr. Hoje said.

"You could put them up. And Mr. Eddy could put up his place too."

"Them two places is worth a plenty more than just five hundred dollars," Mr. Eddy started in to argue.

"Not on the tax books, the way I hear tell from my little green-eyed bird."

Reed Barnitt beckoned us around him again. "Can't we raise it somehow?" he whispered. "We're just before finding a fortune."

Mr. Hoje and Mr. Eddy said nothing.

"Friends, we've as good as got that Ancients' treasure," Reed Barnitt said, and rummaged out money from his pocket—a wadded ten, a five and some ones. "I'll risk my last cent and take it back off the top of whatever we find. You others can do the same."

Mr. Hoje and Mr. Eddy mumbled together a while, and we others watched. Then they turned, both of them, and went to Aram Harnam.

"We'll want a guarantee," said Mr. Hoje.

"Guarantee?" Aram Harnam repeated him. "Oh, I'll guarantee you the light. I'll put it down in writing that it'll show you to what you seek."

"Draw us up some loan papers," said Mr. Eddy, sharp and deep. "Two hundred and fifty dollars loaned to each of us against our places, and a guarantee the light will work, and sixty days of time to pay you back."

Aram Harnam looked at him, then went into the cabin. He fetched out a tablet of paper and an ink bottle and an old stump of a pen. He wrote out two pages, and Mr. Hoje and Mr. Eddy read them over and signed their names.

Then Aram Harnam bade us wait. He went back inside. What he did in yonder took time, and I watched part of it through the door. He mixed stuff in a pot—I thought I smelt sulphur burning, and once something sweet and spicy, like what frankincense must smell like. There was other stuff, and he heated it so it smoked, then worked it with those furry hands. After while he fetched out what he'd made. It was a big rough candle, big around as your wrist and as long as your arm to the elbow. Its wick looked like gray yarn, and the wax of it was dirty brown.

"Light it at midnight," he said, "and carry it forward. It'll go out at the place where your wish is waiting for you. Understand?"

We said we understood.

"Then good day to youins," said Aram Harnam.

None of us felt the need of sleep that night. At eleven o'clock by Mr. Hoje's big silver turnip watch, we started out to cross the ridge to Black Pine Hollow. Clay went ahead, with a lantern. Reed Barnitt followed with the candle. Then me, with my guitar slung on my back because I mostly always carried it, and a grubbing hoe in my hand. Then Mr. Hoje with a spade, and Mr. Eddy last of us all with a crowbar. Sarah Ann watched us from the door, till we got out of her sight.

Not much of a trail led to Black Pine Hollow, for folks don't love to go there. Last night's hoot owls were at it again, and once or twice we heard rattlings to right and left, like big things a-keeping pace with us among the bushes. Down into the hollow we went, while a breeze blew on us, chill for that time of year. I thought, but didn't sing out loud:

> *In the pines, in the pines,*
> *Where the sun never shines,*
> *And I shiver when the wind blows cold. . . .*

"Whereabouts is this mine?" asked Reed Barnitt.

"I can find it better than Clay," called Mr. Hoje, and he pushed ahead and took the lantern. The light shone duller and duller, the way you'd think that moonless night was trying to smother it. Around us crowded the black pines the hollow was named for. Just to comfort myself, I tweaked a silver guitar string, and it rang so loud we all jumped.

"I think this must be it," said Mr. Hoje, after a long, long while.

He turned off through a thick bunch of the blackest-looking pines, and held the lantern high. Hidden behind the trees rose a rock face like a wall, and in the rock was a raggy hole the size of a door. Vines hung down around it, but they looked dead and burnt out. As we stood still and looked, there was a little foot-patter inside.

"Let's hope and pray that ain't a rat," said Clay. "Rats in a mine is plumb bad luck."

"Shoo," said his daddy, "let's hope it ain't nothing worse than a rat."

"I'm going in," Reed Barnitt said through his tight teeth, "and I sure God don't want to go in alone."

We went in together.

Gentlemen, it was so black in that mine you'd think a chunk of coal would show white. Maybe the lantern was smoking; it made just a little puddle of dim glow for us. Reed Barnitt struck a match on his pants and set it to the yarny wick of that five-hundred-dollar candle. It blazed up clean and strong as the very light Reed Barnitt had made in the middle of the star when he cast the spell. We saw where we were.

Seemed as if there'd been a long hallway cut in the dark brown rock, but pieces had fallen down. They lay on top of one another before us, shutting us away from the hall, so we stood in a little space not much bigger than Mr. Hoje's front room. To either side the walls were of the dark brown stone, marked by cutting tools—those Ancients had chopped their way through solid rock—and underfoot lay pebbles. Some were quartz, the way Mr. Hoje had said. All was quiet as the inside of a coffin the night before Judgment Day.

"The flame's pointing," Reed Barnitt called to us.

It did point, like a burning finger, straight into the place. He stepped toward those rocks, that piled into something like steps to go up, and we moved with him. I'll guarantee none of us wanted to go over the rocks and beyond. The blackness behind there made you feel not only nobody had ever been in there, but likewise nobody could ever go; the blackness would shove him back like a hand.

I moved behind Reed Barnitt with the others. The light of the candle shone past his blocky body and wide hat, making him look like something cut out of black cloth. Two-three steps, and he stopped so quick we almost bumped him. "The light flutters," he said.

It did flutter, and now it didn't point to the piled rocks, but to the wall at their right. When Reed Barnitt made a pace that direction, it winked out, we all stood close together in the dim lantern light.

Reed Barnitt put his hand on the rock wall. It

showed ghosty white on the brown. His finger crawled along a seamy crack. "Dig there," he said to us.

By what light the lantern showed, I shoved the pick end of the grubbing hoe into the crack and gouged. Seemed the whole wall fought me, but I heaved hard and the crack widened. It made a heavy spiteful noise somewhere. Mr. Eddy drove in the end of his bar and dragged down.

"Come help me, Clay," he called. "Put your man on this here."

The two pulled down with all their long tall bodies, and then together they pushed up. My heart jumped inside me, for a piece of rock the size of a bed-mattress was moving. I shoved on the hoe handle. Reed Barnitt grabbed the free edge of the moving piece, and all of us laid into it—then jumped back, just in time.

The big loose hunk dropped out like the lid of a box. Underneath was dark dirt. Mr. Eddy drove the crowbar point into it.

"Light that there candle thing again," he told Reed Barnitt.

Reed Barnitt struck a match and tried. "Won't light," he said. "We've found the place. We've got our hand right on it."

I reckon that's the moment we all believed him. So far we'd worried and bothered, but now we stopped that and worked. Clay took the spade from Mr. Hoje, and I swung my hoe. He scooped out the dirt I loosened. We breathed hard, watching or working. Suddenly:

"John," said Clay, "didn't I hear that hoe blade hit metal?"

I slammed it down into the dirt again, hard as I could. Clay scooped out a big spadeful. Bright yellow glimmered up out of the dark dirt. Clay grabbed into it, and so did his daddy. I had my mouth open to yell, but Reed Barnitt yelled first:

"God in the bushes, look up there!"

He had turned away from our work, and he was pointing up those step-piled rocks. On the top rock of them stood something against the choking blackness.

It stood the height of a man, that thing, but you couldn't make sure of its shape. Because it was strung and swaddled over with webby rags. They stirred and fluttered around it, like gray smoke. And it had a hand, and the hand held a skull, with white grinning teeth and eyes that shone.

"It's an Ancient!" Reed Barnitt yelled, and the thing growled deep and hungry and ugly.

Clay dropped his spade. I heard the clank and jingle of metal pieces on the floor pebbles. He gave back, and Mr. Hoje and Mr. Eddy gave back with him. I stood where I was, putting down the hoe. Reed Barnitt was the only one that moved forward.

"Stay clear of us," he sort of breathed out at the raggy-gray thing.

It pushed out the skull at him, and the skull's eyelights blinked and glared. Reed Barnitt backed up.

"Let's get out of here," he choked, "before—"

He hadn't seen us find the treasure, his eyes had been on whatver the thing was. He was for running, but I wasn't.

I'd faced peculiar things before. The Ugly Bird— One Other—and I wouldn't run from that gray thing that held a skull like a lantern.

So I shrugged my guitar in front of me. My left hand grabbed its neck and my right spread on the silver strings, the silver that sudden death to witch doings. I dragged a chord of music from them, and it echoed in there like a whole houseful of guitar-pickers helping me out. I thought the thing up there gave a shudder, and the skull it held wobbled to the side, maybe saying no to me.

"You don't like my music?" I inquired it, and swept out another chord and got my foot on the bottom step-stone.

"Take care, John!" came Reed Barnitt's sick voice.

"Let that thing take care," I told him, and moved up on the rocks.

It flung the skull at me. I dodged, and felt the wind of the skull as it sailed grinning past, and I heard it smash to pieces like a bottle on the rocky floor behind me. For a second that flinging hand stuck out of the gray rags.

I knew whose hand it was, black-furry like a spider.

"Aram Harnam!" I hollered out, and let my guitar drop to swing by its cord, and I charged up those stairs of stones.

Reed Barnitt was after me as I got to the top. I grabbed my both hands full of rags, just as Reed Barnitt clamped onto my arm and dragged me back down. And where the rags had torn away, you could see Aram Harnam's face, all a thicket of hair and beard, with thin nose and shiny eyes.

"What's up?" Mr. Eddy hooted.

"Aram Harnam's up!" I yelled. "He mortgaged your farms to sell us that candle-thing, then came here to scare us out!" I pointed. "And Reed Barnitt's in it with him!"

Reed Barnitt had run up to the top stone and turned around beside Aram Harnam, his eyes big in his white face. I got my feet under me to charge back up at the two of them.

But then I stopped where I was, the way you'd think roots had sprung out of my toes into the rock. There were three up there, not two.

That third one looked at first glimpse like a big, big man wearing a dark fur coat. Then you saw the fur was on the skin, with warty muscles bunching through. The head was more like a frog's than anything else, wide in the mouth and big in the eye and no nose. It spread its arms quiet-like around the shoulders of Reed Barnitt and Aram Harnam, and took hold with two hands that had both claws and webs.

The two men it touched screamed out, like animals

in a snap-trap. They tried to pull free, but those two big shaggy arms just hugged them close and hiked them from their feet. And what had come to fetch them away, it fetched them away, in a blink of time, back into the darkness no sensible soul would dare.

That's when the other four of us up and flung down the lantern and tools and ran like rabbits.

Back at Mr. Hoje's, we lighted the lamp and looked at those two handfuls of metal pieces Clay and Mr. Eddy had grabbed and never turned loose.

"I reckon they're money," said Mr. Hoje, "but I ain't never seen such money as that."

Nary one of us had. They weren't even round, just bumpy-edged and flattened out. You figured they'd been made by putting lumps of soft gold between the jaws of a die and then stamped out. The smallest was bigger and thicker than a four-bit piece. They had figures on them, like men with horned heads and snaky tails, and what might be letters or numbers, only none of us could name what language it was.

We put those coins into an old salt-bag and sat up the rest of the night, not talking any great much but pure down glad of one another's company. We had breakfast together, cooked by Sarah Ann, who had the good sense not to inquire us. After that, came up a young sheriff's deputy.

"Howdy," he said to us. "Ary one of you seen a fellow with a white face and a broad build?"

"What's up with such a one?" asked Mr. Hoje.

"Why, they want him bad at the state prison," said the sheriff's deputy. "He was a show-man, doing play magic, but he took to swindling folks and got in jail and then got out again, and the law's after him."

"We've seen such a man hereabouts," allowed Mr. Eddy, "but he's long gone from here now."

When we were left alone again, we talked how it was. Reed Barnitt did his false tricks like setting that pale light on the star, and writing with invisible ink on the paper so it would show the words when it was heated. And he'd fixed for Aram Harnam to furnish us that candle, to get hold of the property of Mr. Hoje and Mr. Eddy, then scare them so bad they'd never dare look again, and forfeit their home places.

Only:

There *was* treasure there, and those two swindlers never guessed. And something had been left to watch and see it wasn't robbed away.

I don't call to mind which of us said that we'd have to take the gold pieces back, because they'd never do aught of good to honest folks. We went back at noon to Black Pine Hollow. The sun sure enough didn't shine, and we shivered with nary wind blowing.

Inside the mine-mouth, we found the lantern and lighted it. Clay had the nerve to pick up pieces of the broken skull Aram Harnam had flung, and we saw the eyes had shone—pieces of tin in them. We found our spade and hoe and crowbar. Into the hole we flung the gold pieces, on top of what seems a heap more lying there. Then we put back the dirt, tamped it down, and we all heaved and sweated till we'd set the piece of rock in place again.

"The Ancients got their treasure back," said Mr. Hoje, breathing heavily.

Then, noise on those step-stones. I held up the lantern.

Huddled and bent they stood up there, Reed Barnitt and Aram Harnam.

They sort of leaned together, like tired-out horses in plow harness, not quite touching shoulders. Reed Barnitt's white hands and Aram Harnam's shaggy ones hung with the fingers bent and limp. They looked down on us with sad eyes and mouths drooped open, the way you'd think they had some hope about us, but no great much.

"Look," said Clay beside me. "We've given back the gold. They're giving back them two they dragged off last night."

But they looked as if they'd been gone more than a night.

The hair on Reed Barnitt's hatless head was as white as his face. Aram Harnam's beard and the fur on his hands—black no more but a steamy gray. Maybe it had changed from fear, the way folks say can happen. Or maybe there had been *time* for it to change, in that place where they'd been fetched to.

"Go fetch them down, John," Mr. Hoje asked me. "We'll get a doctor for them when we get them to my house."

I started up on the stones with the lantern.

Their eyes picked up the lantern light and shone green, like dog eyes. One of them, I don't know which, made a little whiney cry with no words to it. They ran from me into the dark, and I saw their backs, bent more than I'd thought possible.

I ran up to the top stone and held out the lantern.

I saw them sort of fall forward and run on hands and feet. Like animals. Not quite sure yet of how to run thataway on all fours; but something in me said, mighty positive, they'd learn better as the time went by. I backed down again, without watching any more.

"They won't come out," I said.

Mr. Hoje scuffed his feet on the rock. "From what I seen, I reckon it's as well. They'll stay here with the Ancients."

"The Ancients are dead," spoke up Clay. "Way I reckon, what's in there ain't no Ancients; just something the Ancients left behind. And I don't want no part of it."

From Black Pine Hollow we went to Aram Harnam's empty cabin and there we found the papers he'd tricked Mr. Hoje and Mr. Eddy to sign, and we burned them. On the way back, the two old men made it up betwixt them to spare to Clay and Sarah Ann a few acres from both home places. As to the cabin for the two, neighbors would be proud to help build it.

"One thing wonders me," said Clay. "John, you never had ary notion night before last of singing about the girl with golden slippers on."

"Not till I struck the strings and gave it out," I agreed him.

"Then how came Reed Barnitt just to happen to take them from under his coat for Sarah Ann?" Clay asked of us. "Stage-show magic man or not, how did he just come to do that by chance?"

None of us could reply him.

Sarah Ann kept the golden slippers, and nobody could see a reason why not. I sent on word I'd be late getting to Flornoy College, and stayed around to help build the cabin. Sarah Ann wore the golden slippers at her wedding to Clay, and she danced in them with him while I played song after song, *Pretty Fair Maid* and *Willie from the Western States* and *I Dreamt Last Night of My True Love, All in My Arms I Had Her*. Preacher Crutchfield said the service, what God hath joined together let no man put asunder. And I kissed the pretty-cheeked bride, and so did a many other kind friend, but the only man of us she sure enough kissed back was long tall Clay Herron.

YOU KNOW THE TALE OF HOPH

The noon sun was hot on the thickets, but in his cabin was only blue dim light. His black brows made one streak above his iron-colored eyes. "Yes, ma'am?" he said.

"I'm trying to write a book of stories," she said, and she was rosy-faced, lovely-haired. "I hear you know the tale of Hoph. How sailors threw him off a ship in a terrible storm a hundred years ago, but the sea swept him ashore and then he walked and walked until he reached these mountains. How he troubled the mountain people with spells and curses and sendings of nightmares."

His long white teeth smiled in his long white face. "You seem to know the tale already."

"Not all of it. Why did Hoph torment people?"

"His food was the blood of pretty women," was what he replied her. "Each year he made them give him a pretty woman. When she died at the year's end, with her last drop of blood gone, he made them give him another."

"Until he died, too," she tried to finish.

"He didn't die. They didn't know that he had to be shot with a silver bullet."

Up came his hands into her sight, lean-fingered, crook-nailed.

She screamed once.

From the dark corner where I lay hid I shot Hoph down with a silver bullet.

OLD DEVLINS WAS A-WAITING

Again I was climbing through mountain country. Up from Rebel Creek I'd climbed, and through Lost Cove, and up and down the slopes of Crouch and Hog Ham and Skeleton Ridge, and finally as the sun was hunting the world's western edge once again, I looked over a high saddleback and down on Flornoy College.

Flornoy's up in the hills, plain and poor, but it does good teaching. Country boys who mightn't get much past common school else can come and work off the most part of their board and keep and learning. I saw a couple of brick buildings, a row of cottages, and barns for the college farm in the bottom below, with then a paved road to Hilbertstown maybe eight-nine miles down valley. Climbing down was another sight farther, and longer work than you'd reckon, and when I got to the level it was past sundown and the night showed its first stars to me.

Coming into the back of the college grounds, I saw a light somewhere this side of the buildings, and then I heard two voices quarreling at each other.

"You leave my lantern be," bade one voice, deep and hacked.

"I wasn't going to blow it out, Moon-Eye," the other voice laughed, but sharp and mean. "I just joggled up against it."

"You take care I don't joggle up against you, Rixon Pengraft."

"Maybe you're bigger than me, but there's such a

thing as the difference betwixt a big man and a little one."

Then I was close and saw them, and they saw me. Scholars at Flornoy, I reckoned by the light of the old lantern one of them toted. He was tall, taller than I am, with broad, hunched shoulders, and in the lantern-shine his face looked good in a big-nosed way. The other fellow was plumpy soft, and smoked a cigar that made an orangey coal in the darkening.

That cigar-smoking one turned toward where I came along with my silver-strung guitar in one hand and my old possible-sack in the other.

"What you want around here," he said to me. Didn't ask it—said it.

"I'm looking for Professor Deal," I told him. "Any objections?"

He grinned his teeth white around the cigar. The lantern-shine flickered on them. "None I know of. Go on looking."

He turned and moved off in the night. The fellow with the lantern watched him go, then spoke to me.

"I'll take you to Professor Deal's. My name's Anderson Newlands. Folks call me Moon-Eye."

"Folks call me John," I said. "What does Moon-Eye mean?"

He smiled, sad, over the lantern. "It's hard for me to see in the night-time, John. I was in that Korean war, I got wounded and had a fever, and my eyes began to trouble me. They're getting better, but I need a lantern any night but when it's full moon."

We walked along. "Was that Rixon Pengraft fellow trying to give you a hard time?" I asked.

"Trying, maybe. He—well he wants something I'm not really keeping from him, he just thinks I am."

That's all Moon-Eye Newlands said about it, and I didn't inquire him what he meant. He went on: "I don't want any fuss with Rixon, but if he's bound to have one with me—"

He stopped his talk. "Yonder's Professor Deal's

house, the one with the porch. I'm due there some later tonight, after supper."

He headed off with his lantern, toward the brick building where the scholars slept. On the porch, Professor Deal came out and made me welcome. He's president of Flornoy, middling-tall, with white hair and a round hard chin like a water-washed rock.

"Haven't seen you since the State Fair," he boomed out, loud enough to be heard by the seventy-eighty Flornoy scholars all at once. "Come in the house, John, Mrs. Deal's nearly ready with supper. I want you to meet Dr. McCoy."

I came in and rested my guitar and sack and hat by the door. "Is he a medicine doctor or a teacher doctor?"

"She's a lady. Dr. Anda Lee McCoy. She observes how people think and how far they see."

"An eye-doctor?" I asked.

"Call her an inner-eye doctor, John. She studies what those Duke University people call ESP—extra-sensory perception."

I'd heard tell of that. A fellow named Rhine says folks can some way tell what other folks think in their hearts. He says that everybody reads minds a little, and some folks read them a right much. Might could be you've seen his cards, marked the five ways—square, cross, circle, star, wavy lines. Take five of each and you've got a pack of twenty-five. Somebody shuffles them like for a game and looks at them one by one. Then somebody else who can't see the cards, maybe in the next room, tries to guess what's on them. Ordinary chance is one right guess out of five. But here and there it gets called another sight oftener.

"Some old mountain folks would say that's witching," I said to Professor Deal.

"Hypnotism was called witchcraft until it was shown to be a true science," he said back. "Or telling what dreams mean, and then Dr. Freud made it scientific. ESP may be a recognized science some day soon."

"Do you hold with it, Professor?"

"I hold with anything that's proven," he said. "I'm not sure yet about ESP. Oh, here's Mrs. Deal."

She's a comfortable, clever lady, as white-haired as he is. While I was making my manners, Dr. Anda Lee McCoy came from the back of the house.

"Are you the ballad-singer?" she inquired me.

I'd expected no doctor lady as young or pretty-looking as Dr. Anda Lee McCoy. She was small and slim, but there was enough of her. She stood straight and wore good town clothes, and had lots of yellow hair and a round happy face and straight-looking blue eyes.

"Professor Deal bade me come see him," I said. "He couldn't get Mr. Bascom Lamar Lunsford there to decide something or other about folk songs and tales."

"I'm glad you came," she welcomed me.

Turned out she knew Mr. Bascom well, and thought a right much of him. Professor Deal had asked for him first, but Mr. Bascom was in Washington, a-making records of his songs for the Library of Congress. Some folks can't vote which they'd rather hear, Mr. Bascom's five-string banjo or my guitar; but he knows more old-timey songs than I do, a few more.

Mrs. Deal went to the kitchen to see was supper near about cooked. We others sat down in the front room. Dr. McCoy asked me to sing, so I got my guitar and gave her *Shiver in the Pines*, from where I'd lately been.

"Pretty," she praised. "Do you know a song about killing a captain by a lonesome river ford."

I thought. "Some of it, yes, ma'am. That's a Virginia song, I reckon. Do you relish it?"

"I wasn't thinking of my own taste. A student here, a man named Anderson Newlands, doesn't like it at all."

Mrs. Deal bade us to supper, and while we ate Dr. McCoy talked. "I'll tell you why I'm glad you're here, John," she said. "I've got a theory, or a hypothesis. About dreams."

"Not quite like Freud," added on Professor Deal, "though he'd be interested if he was alive and here."

"It's about dreaming the future," said Dr. McCoy.

"Shoo," I said, "that's no theory, that's fact. Bible folks did it. I've done it myself. Once, during the war—"

But that was no tale to tell, what I'd dreamed in war time and how true it came out. So I held my peace, and Dr. McCoy went on:

"There are records of prophecies coming true, even after the prophets died. And another set of records fit in, about images appearing like ghosts. Most of these are ancestors of someone alive today. Kinship and special sympathy, you know. Perhaps these images, or ghosts, are called from the past by using diagrams and spells. You aren't laughing at me, John?"

"No, ma'am. Things like that aren't apt to be a laughing matter."

"What if dreams of the future come true because somebody goes forward in time while he sleeps or drowses?" she inquired us. "That ghost of Nostradamus, reported not long ago—what if Nostradamus himself came into this present time, then went back to his own century to set down a prophecy of what he'd seen?"

If she wanted an answer, I'd none to give her. I only said: "Do you want to call somebody from the past, ma'am? Or maybe go yourself into a time that's coming?"

She shook her yellow head.

"Putting it one way, John, I'm not psychic. Putting it another way, the scientific way, I'm not adapted. But this young man, Anderson Newlands, is the best adapted I've ever found."

She told how some Flornoy scholars scored high at guessing the cards and their markings. I was right interested that Rixon Pengraft called them well, though Dr. McCoy said his mind got on other things—I reckon his mind got on her; pretty thing as she was, she'd take a man's mind. But Anderson Newlands, Moon-Eye Newlands, called every card right as she held the pack, time and time again, with nary miss.

"And he dreams of the future, he says," she added on. "If he can see the future, he might call to the past."

"By the diagrams and the words?" I inquired her. "How about the science explanation for that?"

She had one, and told it while we ate our custard pie.

First, the notion that time's the fourth dimension. You're six feet tall, twenty inches wide, twelve inches thick and thirty-five years old; and the thirty-five years of you reach from where you were born one place across the land and maybe over the sea where you've traveled, and finally to right where you are now, from thousands of miles ago. Then the notion that just a dot drawn here in this second of time we live in can be part of a wire back and back and forever back, or a five-inch line is a five-inch bar reaching forever back thataway, or a circle is a tube and so on. It made some sense to me, and I asked Dr. McCoy what it added up to.

It added up to the diagram witch-folks draw, with circles and stars and letters from an alphabet nobody on this earth can spell out. That diagram might could be a cross-section, here in our three dimensions, of something reaching backward and forward, a machine to travel you through time.

"These are only guesses," she said, and smiled and then frowned. "The way I might guess with the ESP cards. But I'd like to find whether the right man could call his ancestor out of the past.

"I still don't make out about those spoken spells the witch-folks use," I said, remembering Mr. Howsen and Miss Annalinda and the false magic man Reed Barnitt.

"A special sound can start a machine," said Professor Deal. "I've seen such things."

"Like the words of the old magic square?" asked Dr. McCoy. "The one they used in spells to call up the dead?"

She got a pencil and scrap of paper, and wrote it out:

```
S A T O R
A R E P O
T E N E T
O P E R A
R O T A S
```

"I've seen that for a many years," I said. "The witch people use it, and it's in witch books like *The Long Lost Friend*."

"You'll notice," said Dr. McCoy, "that it reads the same, whether you start at the upper left and read down word by word, or at the lower right and read backward and upward; or if you read it straight down or straight up."

Porfessor Deal looked, too. "The first two words, SATOR and AREPO, are reversals of the last two. SATOR for ROTAS, and AREPO for OPERA.

"I've worked that out," I braved up to say. "The first two words being the last two, turned round. But the third, fourth and fifth are sure-enough words—I've heard tell that TENET means *faith* and OPERA is *works*, and ROTAS might could mean something about wheels."

"But SATOR and AREPO are more than just reversed words," Professor Deal said. "I'm no great Latinist, but I know that SATOR means a *sower*—planter —or a beginner or creator."

"Creator." Dr. McCoy jumped on his last word. "That would fit into this if it's a real sentence."

"A sentence and a palindrome," nodded Professor Deal. "Know what a palindrome is, John?"

"A sentence that reads the same back and forward," I said. "Like Napoleon saying *Able was I ere I saw*

Elba, or the first words Eve heard in the Garden of Eden, *Madam, I'm Adam*. Those are old grandsire jokes to pleasure young children."

"If this is a sentence, it's more than a palindrome," said Dr. McCoy. "It's a double palindrome, because it reads the same from any point you start—backward, forward, up or down. Fourfold meaning would be fourfold power as a spell or formula."

"But what's the meaning?" I still wanted to know.

She began to write on the paper. "SATOR," she said out loud, "*the creator*. Whether that's the creator of a machine or the Creator of all things—I suppose it's a machine-creator."

"Likely," I agreed her, "because this doesn't sound to me the kind of way the Creator of all things does His works."

Mrs. Deal smiled and excused herself. We could talk, she said, but she had sewing to do.

"AREPO," Professor Deal kind of hummed to himself. "I wish I had a Latin dictionary, though even then I might not find it. Maybe that's a corruption of *repo* or *crepo*, to crawl or climb—a vulgar form of the word."

I said naught. I hadn't reckoned Professor Deal would say a vulgar thing in front of a lady. But all Dr. McCoy remarked him was: "AREPO—wouldn't that be a noun ablative? By means of?"

"Write it down like that," said Professor Deal. "*By means of creeping, climbing, by means of great effort*. And TENET is the verb *to hold*. He holds, *the creator holds*."

"OPERA is *works*, and ROTAS is *wheels*," Dr. McCoy tried to finish up.

"ROTAS probably is accusative plural, in apposition," nodded Professor Deal. "Maybe we'll never be sure, but let's read it like this: *The creator, by great effort, holds the wheels for his works*."

I'd not said a word to all this scholar-talk, till then. "TENET might could still be faith," I offered them.

"Faith's needed to help any workings. Folks without faith would call the whole thing foolishness."

"That's sound psychology," said Professor Deal.

"And it fits with the making of spells," Dr. McCoy added on. "Double meaning all along—or triple or fourfold meanings, all of them adding truth." She read from the paper: "*'The creator, by great effort, holds the wheels for his works.'*"

"It might refer to the orbits of planets," Professor Deal said.

"Or to the making of a diagram, as a reference point in this instant of time on some time-traveling machine," argued Dr. McCoy.

"Where do I come in?" I asked.

"You can sing something for us," Dr. McCoy replied me, "and you can have that faith you were talking about."

A knock at the door, and Professor Deal went to let the visitor in. Moon-Eye Newlands hiked his lantern chimney and blew out the light. He looked tall, the way he'd looked when first I met him in the outside dark, and he had on a white shirt with a black tie and blue pants. He smiled, friendly, and moon-eyed or not he looked first of all at Dr. McCoy, clear and honest and glad to see her.

"You said you wanted me to help you, Doctor," he greeted her.

"Thank you, Mr. Newlands," she said, gentler and warmer than I'd heard her so far.

"You can call me Moon-Eye, like everybody else."

He was a college scholar and she was a doctor-lady, but they were near about the same age. I recollected he'd been off to the Korean war.

"Shall we go out on the porch?" Dr. McCoy asked us. "Professor Deal says I can draw my diagram there. Bring your guitar, John."

We went out. Moon-Eye lighted his lantern again, and Dr. McCoy kneeled down to draw with a piece of chalk. First she made the word square, big letters:

```
S A T O R
A R E P O
T E N E T
O P E R A
R O T A S
```

Around these she made a triangle, a good three feet from base to point. Then another triangle across it, pointing the other way to make what learned folks call the Star of David. Around that a big circle, with writing along the edge of it, and another big circle around that to close in the writing. From where I sat with my back to a porch post, I could read the word square all right, but of the writing between the circles I couldn't spell ary letter.

"Folks," said Moon-Eye, "I still can't say I like this."

Kneeling to draw, Dr. McCoy looked up at him with her blue eyes. "You said you'd help me if you could."

"But what if it's not right? My old folks, my grandsires, I can't rightly say if they ought to be called up."

"Moon-Eye," said Professor Deal, "I'm just watching, observing. I haven't yet been convinced of anything due to happen here tonight. But if it does happen—I'm sure your ancestors were nobody to be ashamed of, dead or alive."

"I'm not ashamed of them," Moon-Eye told us all, with a sort of clip in his voice. "I just don't think they were the sort to be stirred up without good reason."

"Moon-Eye," said Dr. McCoy, talking the way any man who's a man would want a woman to talk to him, "science is the best of reasons in itself."

He didn't speak, didn't nod his head or either shake it. He just looked at her blue eyes with his dark ones. She got up from where she kneeled.

"John," she spoke to where I sat, "that song we mentioned. About the lonesome river ford. It might put things in the right mood and tempo."

Moon-Eye sat on the edge of the porch, his lantern

by him. Its light made our shadows big and jumpy. I picked the tune and sang:

> "Old Devlins was a-waiting
> By the lonesome river ford,
> When he spied the Mackey captain
> With a pistol and a sword..."

"I stopped, for Moon-Eye had drawn himself tight. "I'm not certain sure how it goes from there," I excused myself.

"I'm sure how it goes," said someone in the dark, and up to the porch ambled Rixon Pengraft.

He was a-smoking that cigar, or a fresh one, grinning round it. He wore a brown corduroy shirt with officers' straps to the shoulders, and brown corduroy pants tucked into shiny half-boots worth maybe thirty dollars the pair of them. His hair was brown, too, and curly, and his eyes sneaked all over Dr. Anda Lee McCoy.

"Nobody here knows what that song means," said Moon-Eye.

Rixon Pengraft sat down beside Dr. McCoy, on the step below Moon-Eye, and the way he did it made me hark back in my mind to a thing Moon-Eye had said; about something Rixon Pengraf wanted, and why he hated Moon-Eye over it.

"I've wondered wasn't the song about the Confederate War," said Rixon. "Maybe Mackey captain means Yankee captain."

"No, it doesn't," said Moon-Eye, and his teeth clicked together.

"Anyway, I'll sing it," said Rixon, twiddling his cigar in his mouth and winking at Dr. McCoy. "Go on picking."

"Go on picking," Dr. McCoy repeated, and Moon-Eye said nothing. I touched the silver strings, and Rixon Pengraft sang:

"Old Devlins, Old Devlins,
I know you mighty well,
You're six foot three of Satan,
Two hundred pounds of hell—"

He stopped. "Devlins—Satan," he said. "Maybe it's a song about Satan. Think we ought to sing about him with no proper respect?"

He went on:

"Old Devlins was ready,
He feared not beast or man,
He shot the sword and pistol
From the Mackey captain's hand."

Moon-Eye looked once at the diagram chalked out on the floor of the porch. He didn't seem to hear Rixon Pengraft's mocking voice with the next verse:

"'Old Devlins, Old Devlins,
Oh, won't you spare my life?
I've got three little children
And a kind and loving wife.'"

"'God bless your little children
And I'm sorry for your wife,
But turn your back and close your eyes,
I'm going to take your—'"

"Hush up that singing!" yelled Moon-Eye Newlands.

And he was on his feet in the yard, so quick we hadn't seen him move. He took a long step toward where Rixon Pengraft sat beside Dr. McCoy, and Rixon got up quick, too, and dropped his cigar and moved away.

"You know the song," said Moon-Eye. "Maybe you guess what man you're singing about!"

"Maybe I do," said Rixon.

"Do you want to fetch him here to look on you?"

We were all up on our feet now. We watched Moon-Eye standing over Rixon, and just then Moon-Eye looked about two feet taller than he'd looked before. Maybe even more than that, to Rixon.

"Well, if that's how you're going to be—" began Rixon.

"That's how I'm going to be," Moon-Eye said, his voice right quiet again. "I'm honest to tell you, that's how I'm going to be."

"Then I won't stay here," said Rixon. "I'll leave, because you're making so much noise in front of a lady. But, Moon-Eye, I'm not scared of you. Nor yet am I scared of the ghost of any ancestor you ever had, if his name's Devlins or aught else."

Rixon smiled at Dr. McCoy and went walking away. We heard him start to whistle in the dark. He meant it for banter, but I couldn't help but think about the boy whistling his way through the graveyard.

Then I just happened to look back on the diagram chalked on the porch floor. And it didn't seem right for a moment: it looked like something else. The two circles, with the string of writing between them, the six-pointy star, and in the very middle of everything the word square:

```
    S A T O R
    A R E P O
    T E N E T
    O P E R A
    R O T A S
```
(shown reversed/upside-down)

"Shoo," I said. "Look there, folks, that word square's turned round."

"Naturally," said Professor Deal, plain glad to talk and think about something besides how Moon-Eye and Rixon had acted. "The first two words are reversals of the—"

"I don't mean that, Professor." I pointed. "Look. I take my Bile oath that Dr. McCoy wrote it out so that it read rightly from where I am now. But it's turned upside down."

"That's the pure truth," Moon-Eye agreed me.

"Yes," said Dr. McCoy. "Yes, you know what that means?"

"The square's turned around?" asked Professor Deal.

"The whole thing's turned around. The whole diagram. Spun a whole hundred and eighty degrees—maybe spun several times. Why?" She put her hand on Moon-Eye's arm, and the hand trembled. "The thing was beginning to work. The machine was going to operate."

"That's right." Moon-Eye put his hand over her little one, just a moment. "Then the singing stopped, and it stopped too."

He moved away from her and picked up his lantern and started away.

"Come back, Moon-Eye!" she called to him. "It can't work without you."

"I've got something to see Rixon Pengraft about," he said.

"You can't hit him, you're bigger than he is!"

I thought she'd go running to catch him up. "Stay here," I told her. "I'll go talk to him."

I walked quick to catch up with Moon-Eye. "Big things were near bout to happen just now," I said.

"I realize that, Mr. John. But it won't go on, because I won't be there to help." He lifted his lantern and stared at me. "I said my old folks weren't the sort you can wake up for no reason."

"Was that song about your old folks?"

"Sort of."

"You mean, Old Devlins?"

"That's not exactly his name, but he was my great-grandsire on my mother's side. Rixon Pengraft guesses that, and after what he said—"

"You heard the doctor-lady say Rixon's littler than

you are," I argued him. "If you hit him, she won't like it."

He stalked on toward the brick building where the scholars had their rooms.

Bang!

The lantern went out with a smash of glass.

The two of us stopped still in the dark. Up ahead, in the brick building, a head made itself black in a lighted window and a cigar-coal glowed.

"I said I don't fear you, Moon-Eye!" laughed Rixon Pengraft. "And I don't fear Old Devlins, whatever kin he is to you!"

A black arm waved something. It was a rifle. Moon-Eye drew himself up tall in the night.

"Help me, Mr. John," he said. "I can't see a hand before me."

"You going to fight him, Moon-Eye? When he's got that gun?"

"Help me back to Professor Deal's." His hand gripped down on my shoulder. "Get me into the light."

"What do you aim to do?"

"Something there wasn't any reason to do, till now."

That's the last the either of us said. We walked back. Nobody was on the porch, but the door was open. We stepped across the chalk diagram and into the front room. Professor Deal and Dr. McCoy stood looking at us.

"You've come back," Dr. McCoy said to Moon-Eye, the gladdest you'd ever call for a lady to sound. She stepped toward him and put out her hand. "I heard a gun out there," she said.

"My lantern got shot to pieces," Moon-Eye told her. "I've come back to do what you want. Mr. John, if you don't know the song—"

"I know it, Moon-Eye," I said. "I stopped because I thought you didn't want it."

"I want it now," his voice rang out. "If my great-grandsire can be called here tonight, call him. Sing that song."

I slanted my guitar across me and picked the strings:

> "He killed the Mackey captain,
> He went behind the hill,
> The Mackeys never caught him,
> And I guess they never will...."

"Great-grandsire!" cried Moon-Eye, so that the walls shook with the cry. "I've taken a right much around here, because I thought it would be best thataway. But tonight Rixon Pengraft dared you, said he didn't fear you! Come and show him what it is to be afraid!"

"Now, now—" began Professor Deal, then stopped it.

I sang on:

> "When there's no moon in heaven
> And you hear the hound-dogs bark,
> You can guess that it's Old Devlins
> A-scrambling in the dark...."

Far off outside, a hound-dog barked in the moonless night.

And on the door there sounded a thumpety-bank knock, the way you'd think the hand that knocked had knuckles of mountain flint.

I saw Dr. McCoy weave and sway on her little feet like a bush in a wind, and her blue eyes got the biggest they'd been yet. But Moon-Eye just smiled, hard and sure, as Professor Deal walked to the door and opened.

Next moment he sort of swallowed in his throat and tried to shove the door shut again, but he wasn't quick enough. A wide hat with a long dark beard under it pushed in at the door, then big, hunched shoulders like Moon-Eye's. And, spite of all the Professor's shoving, the door came open all the way, and in slid the long-bearded, big-shouldered man among us.

He stood without moving, inside the door. He was six feet three, all right, and I reckoned he'd weigh at two hundred pounds.

He wore a frocktail coat and knee boots of cowhide. His left arm cradled a rifle gun near about as long as he was, and its barrel was eight-square, the way you hardly see any more. His big right hand came up and peeled off the wide hat.

Then we saw his face, such a face as I'm not likely to forget. Big nose and bright glaring eyes, and that beard I tell you about, that fell like a curtain from the high cheekbones and from just under the nose. Wild, he looked, and proud, and deadly as his weight in blasting powder with the fuse already a-spitting. I reckon that old Stonewall Jackson might could have had somewhat of that favor, if ever he'd turned his back on the Lord.

"I thought I dreamt this," he said, deep as somebody talking from a well-bottom, "but I begin to figure the dream's come true."

His terrible eyes came around to me, shining like two drawn knives.

"You named me a certain name in your song," he said. "I've been made mad by that name on the wrong mouth."

"Devlins?" I said.

"Devil Anse," and he nodded. "The McCoy crowd named me that. My right name's Captain Anderson Hatfield, and I hear tell that somebody round here took a shot at my great-grandboy." He studied Moon-Eye. "That's you, ain't it, son?"

"Now wait, whoever you are—" began Professor Deal.

"I'm Captain Anderson Hatfield," he said again, and the butt of his gun thumped down on the floor like a tree falling.

"I didn't hear any shooting," yammered Professor Deal.

"I heared it," said Devil Anse, "and likewise I heared the slight put on me by the shooter."

"I don't want any trouble," the Professor tried to argue.

"Nor you won't have none, if you hark at me," said Devil Anse. "Look out yonder."

We looked out at the open door. Just next the porch stood the shadows of three men, tall, wide-hatted, leaning on their rifles.

"Since I was obliged to come," said Devil Anse Hatfield, "I didn't come alone." He spoke into the night. "Jonce?"

"Yes, Pa."

"You'll be running things here. You and Vic and Cotton Top keep your eyes on this here house. Nobody's to go from it, for the law nor for aught else."

"Yes, Pa."

We looked at Devil Anse Hatfield, and thought about who he'd been.

All those years back, sixty of them, seventy, we thought to the Big Sandy that flows between West Virginia and Kentucky. And the fighting betwixt the Hatfields and the McCoys, over what beginning nobody can rightly say today, but fighting that brought blood and death and sorrow to all that part of the world. And the trying to make it cease, by all manner of arguers and law officers, who couldn't keep the Hatfields and the McCoys apart from one another's throats. And there he was, Devil Anse Hatfield, from that other time and place, turning to pick me out with his eye.

"You who sung the song," he said. "Come with me."

I put down my guitar. "Proud to come with you, Captain."

He gripped his hand on my shoulder the way Moon-Eye had, a bear-trap grip. We walked out the door, and off the porch past the three tall waiting shadows, and on across the grounds in the night toward that tall brick building where the scholars stayed.

"You know where we're bound?" I inquired him.

"Seems to me I do. What's your name?"

"John," I said.

"John, I left Moon-Eye back yonder because he

called me to come tend to things. He felt it was for me to talk to that fellow. I can't put tongue to his name right off."

"Rixon Pengraft?"

"Rixon Pengraft," he repeated me. "I dreamt that name. Here we are, open that there door for us."

I'd never been in that building, nor either had Devil Anse Hatfield, except maybe in what dreams had fetched him there. But if he'd found his way from the long ago, he found his way to where he was headed. We walked along the hall inside, betwixt doors, till he stopped me at one. "Knock," he said, and I put my fist to the wood.

A mean, shaky laugh inside. "That you, Moon-Eye Newlands?" asked Rixon Pengraft's voice. "You think you dare come in here? All right, the door's unlocked. Turn the knob if you dare."

Devil Anse nudged my shoulder. I opened the door and shoved it in, and we came across the sill together.

Rixon sat on his bed, with a little old twenty-two across his lap.

"Glad you did have the nerve, Moon-Eye," he began to say, "because there's only room for one of us to sit next to Anda Lee McCoy—"

Then his mouth stayed open, with no more words to come out.

"You know who I am?" said Devil Anse.

Rixon's eyes hung out of his head like two scuppernong grapes on a vine. They twitchy-climbed up Devil Anse, from his big boots to his hat, and they got bigger and scareder all the time.

"I don't believe it," said Rixon, almost too sick and weak for an ear to hear him.

"You'd better start in to believe it. You sung about me. Named me Devil Anse in the song, and you knowed it was about me. You thought it would be right amusing if I come where you was."

At last that big hand quit my shoulder, and that long eight-square rifle came to the ready.

"Don't!"

Rixon was on his knees, and his little toy gun spilled on the floor toward us. He was believing now.

"Listen," Rixon jibber-jabbered, "I didn't mean anything. It was just a joke on Moon-Eye."

"A sorry joke," said Devil Anse. "I ain't never yet laughed at a gun going off." His boot-toe shoved at the twenty-two. "Not even a baby child's gun like that."

"I—" Rixon tried to say, and he had to stop to get his strength. "I'll—"

"You'll break up that there gun," Devil Anse decreed him.

"Break my gun?" Rixon was still on his knees, but his scared eyes got an argue look.

"Break it," said Devil Anse. "I'm a-waiting, Rixon, just like that time I waited by the lonesome river ford."

And his words were as cold and slow and hard as chunks of ice floating along a half-choked stream in winter.

Rixon reached his hand for the twenty-two. His eyes couldn't quit hold on Devil Anse. Rixon lifted one knee from the floor and laid the twenty-two across. He tugged at barrel and stock.

"Harder than that," said Devil Anse. "Show us if you got any muscle to match your loud mouth."

Rixon tugged again, and then Devil Anse's rifle stirred. Rixon saw, and really tugged. The little rifle broke at the balance. I heard the wood crack and splinter.

"All right," said Devil Anse, still cold and slow and hard. "You're done with them jokes you think's so funny. Fling them chunks of gun out yonder."

He wagged his head at the open door, and Rixon flung the broken pieces into the hall.

"Stay on your knees," Devil Anse ordered him. "You got some praying to do. Pray the good Lord your thanks that you got off so lucky. Because if there's another time you see me, I'll be the last thing you see this side of the hell I'm two hundred pounds of."

To me he said: "Come on, John. We're done with this here no-excuse for a man who's broke his own gun."

Back we went, with nary word betwixt us. The other three Hatfields stood by Professor Deal's porch, three quiet shadows of three gun-carrying men. In at the door we walked, and there was Professor Deal, and over against the room's other side stood Moon-Eye and Dr. McCoy.

"Rixon named somebody in here a McCoy," said Devil Anse, like Satan himself calling for a lost soul. "Who owns up to the name?"

"I do," said she, gentle but steady.

"You just hold away from her, Great-grandsire," spoke up Moon-Eye.

"Boy," said Devil Anse, "you telling me what to do and not do?"

"I'm telling you, Great-grandsire."

I stood looking at these two tall, big-nosed men from two times in the same family's history, and, saving Devil Anse's dark curtain of beard, you couldn't call for two who favored one another's looks any more.

"Boy," said Devil Anse, "you trying to scare me?"

"No, Great-grandsire. From what I've heard, you can't be scared."

Devil Anse smiled. His smile made his face look the terriblest he'd looked so far that night.

"Now, it's good you heard that, because it's the truth," he said to Moon-Eye.

"I'm just telling you to hold away from her, Great-grandsire."

Dr. McCoy was standing close to Moon-Eye, and as Moon-Eye spoke he put up his arm and set it around her and drew her closer still.

Devil Anse put his awful eyes on them, and that

scary smile crawled away out of his beard like a bad poison snake out of grass and we saw it no more.

"Great-grandboy," he said, "it wasn't needful for you to get me told. You hark at me now; once I made a mistake about a McCoy girl, Jonce—he's my son, standing right out yonder this minute—Jonce loved her and courted her for his own. Her name was Roseanna."

"Roseanna," a voice outside repeated him, said the name oh so sad and so sweet and so lonesome.

"I never give them the leave to marry," said Devil Anse. "Wish I had, now. It'd have saved a sight of trouble and grief and killing. And ain't nobody yet never heard me say that."

His eyes had quit their awfulness, a trifle, and they relished Dr. McCoy, and then how it amazed me to see how they could be quiet eyes, kind eyes.

"Girl," he said, "even if you're aught of close kin to old Ran McCoy hisself—"

"I'm not sure of the relationship," she said. "It's there somewhere, and I'm not ashamed of it."

"Nor you needn't never be." His beard went down and up as he nodded at her. "I fit the McCoy set for long years of my life, and not never once did I find ary scared soul amongst them. Ain't no least tiny drop of coward blood in their veins."

He turned. "I'll be going," he said.

"Going?" asked Professor Deal.

"Yes, sir. Got a right far piece to go. Good night to the all of youins."

He went out through the door, hat, beard and rifle, and closed it behind him, and off far again we could hear the hound-dog bark.

We were as quiet as dead hogs there in the room. Finally.

"Well, God bless my soul!" said Professor Deal, and he wasn't cursing.

"It truly happened," I said.

"But it won't be believed. John. No sane person will ever believe, who wasn't here."

I turned to say something to Moon-Eye and Dr. McCoy. But they were looking deep at each other, and Moon-Eye's both arms were round about that doctor-lady, and her both arms were round about Moon-Eye. And if I'd said whatever I'd had in mind to say, I don't reckon they'd have harked at me.

Mrs. Deal said something from that room where she'd gone to do her sewing, and Professor Deal walked in there to join her. I felt I might could be one too many, too, just then. I picked up my silver-strung guitar and went outside after Devil Anse Hatfield.

He wasn't there, nor yet those who'd come with him. But on the porch was the chalk diagram, and I had light enough to see that the word square read right side up again, the way it had been first set down by Dr. Anda Lee McCoy.

McCoy—Mackey. Devlins—Devil Anse. Names change in the old songs, but what they mean stays there.

Naturally, the way my habit is, I began to pick at my silver strings, another song I'd heard from time to time as I'd wandered up the hills and down the hollows:

"High on the top of the mountain,
  Away from the sins of this world,
  Anse Hatfield's son, he laid down his gun
  And dreamt about Ran McCoy's girl. . . ."

FIND THE PLACE YOURSELF

It might could be true there's a curse on that house. It's up a mountain cove not many know of, and those who do know won't talk to you about it. So if you want to go there you'll have to find the place yourself.

When you find it you won't think at first it's any great much. Just a little house, half logs and half whipsawed planks, standing quiet and gray and dry, the open door daring you to come in.

But don't you go taking such a dare. Nor don't look too long at the three different-colored flowers on the bush by the doorstone. Those flowers look back at you like faces, with eyes that hold your eyes past the breaking away.

In the trees over you will be wings flapping, but not bird wings. Roundabout you will sound voices, so soft and faint they're like voices you recollect from some long-ago time, saying things you wish you could leave forgotten.

If you get past the place, look back and you'll see the path wiggle behind you like a snake after a lizard. Then's when to run like a lizard, run your fastest and hope it's fast enough.

THE DESRICK ON YANDRO

The folks at the party clapped me such an encore, I sang that song.

The lady had stopped her car when she saw my thumb out and my silver-strung guitar under my arm. Asked where I was headed, I told her nowhere special. Asked could I play the guitar, I played it as we rolled along. Asked me my name, I told her John. Then she invited me, most kindly, to her big country house to sing to her friends. They'd be obliged, she said. So I went there with her.

The people were fired up with what they'd drunk, lots of ladies and men in costly clothes, and I had my bothers not getting drunk myself. But, too, they liked what I played and sang. Staying off the worn-out songs, I smote out what they'd never heard before —*Rebel Soldier* and *Well I Know That Love Is Pretty* and *When the Stars Begin to Fall*. When they clapped me and hollered me for more, I sang the Yandro song, like this:

> "I'll build me a desrick on Yandro's high hill
> Where the wild beasts can't reach me nor hear my sad cry,
> For you've gone away, gone to stay a while,
> But you'll come back if you come ten thousand miles . . ."

Then they strung all round and made me more welcome than just any stranger could call for, and the hostess lady said I must stay for supper and sleep there that night. But at that moment, everybody sort of pulled back, and one man came up and sat down by me.

I'd been aware that, when first he came in, things stilled down. It was like when a big bully shows himself among little boys. He was built short and broad, his clothes were cut handsome and costly. His buckskin hair was combed across his head to baffle folks he wasn't getting bald. His round pink face wasn't soft, and his big smiling teeth reminded you he had a skull under the meat. His pale eyes, like two gravel bits, made me recollect I needed a haircut and a shoe shine.

"You said Yandro, young man," said this fellow, almost like a charge in court, with me the prisoner.

"Yes, sir. The song's not too far from the Smokies. I heard it in a valley, and the highest peak over that valley's named Yandro. Now," I said, "I've had scholar-folks argue me it really means yonder, yonder high hill. But the peak's named Yandro, not a usual name."

"No," and he smiled toothy and fierce, "not a usual name. I'm like the peak. I'm named Yandro, too."

"How you, Mr. Yandro?" I said.

"I've never heard of that valley or peak, nor, I imagine, did my father. But my grandfather—Joris Yandro—came from the Southern mountains. He was young, with small education, but lots of energy and ambition." Mr. Yandro swelled up inside his fancy clothes. "He went to New York, then Chicago. His fortunes prospered. His son—my father—and then I, we contrived to make them prosper still more."

"You're to be honored," I said, my politest; but I judged, with no sure reason, that he might could not be too honorable about how he made his money, or either used it. How the others pulled back from him made me reckon he scared them, and that breed of folks scares worst where their money-pocket's located.

"I've done all right," he said, not caring who heard

the brag. "I don't think anybody for a hundred miles around here can turn a deal or make a promise without asking me first. John, I own this part of the world."

Again he showed his teeth.

"You're the first one ever to tell me where my grandfather might have come from. Yandro's high hill, eh? How do we get there, John?"

I tried to recollect the way from highway to side way, side way to trail, and so in and round and over. "I fear I could show you better than I could tell you," I said.

"All right, you'll show me," he said, with no notion I might could have something different to do. "I can afford to make up my mind on a moment's notice, like that. I'll call the airport and charter a plane and we'll leave right now."

"I've asked John to stay here tonight," said my hostess lady.

"We leave now," said Mr. Yandro, and she hushed right up, and I saw how everybody was scared of him. Maybe they'd be pleasured if I got him out of there for a spell.

"Get your plane," I said. "I'll go with you."

He meant that thing he'd said. Not many hours had died before the hired plane set us down at the airport betwixt Asheville and Hendersonville. A taxi rode us into Hendersonville. Mr. Yandro found a used car man still at his place, and bought a fair car from him. Then, on my guiding, Mr. Yandro took out in the dark for that part of the mountains I told him about.

The sky stretched over us with no moon at all, only a many stars like little stitches of blazing thread in a black quilt. For sure-enough light, only our headlamps—first on a paved road twining round one slope and over another and behind a third, then a pretty good gravel road, then a pretty bad dirt road.

"What a stinking country!" said Mr. Yandro as we

chugged along a ridge top as lean as a butcher knife.

I didn't say how I resented that word about a country that stoops to none on earth for prettiness. "Maybe we should ought to have waited for daytime," was all I said.

"I don't ever wait," he sniffed. "Where's the town?"

"There's nary town. Just the valley. Three-four hours away, I judge. We'll be there by midnight."

"Oh, God. Let's have some more of that whiskey I brought," and he reached for the glove compartment, but I pushed his hand away.

"Not if you're driving these mountain roads, Mr. Yandro."

"Then you drive and I'll take a drink."

"I don't know how to drive a car."

"Oh, God," he said again, and couldn't have scorned me more if I'd said I didn't know how to wash my face. "What's a desrick, exactly?"

"That's a word only old-timey folks use these days. It's the kind of cabin they used to make, strong logs and a door you can bar, and loophole windows. So maybe you might could stand off Indians."

"Or the wild beasts can't reach you," he quoted, and snickered. "What wild beasts do you have up here in the Forgotten Latitudes?"

"Can't rightly say all of them. A few bears, a wildcat or two. Used to be wolves, and a bounty for killing them. And so on."

True enough, I wasn't certain sure about the tales I'd heard, and didn't love to tell them if Mr. Yandro would say they were foolish for the lack of sense.

The narrow road climbed a great rocky slant one way, then doubled back to climb the other way, and petered out into just a double rut with an empty, scary-as-hell drop thousands of feet beside the car. Finally Mr. Yandro edged us onto a sort of notch beside the trail and cut off the power. He shook. Fear must have been a new feel to his bones.

"Want some of this whiskey, John?" he asked, and drank.

"No, I thank you. We walk from here, anyway. Beyond's the valley."

He grumped about that, but out he got. I took a flashlight and my guitar and led out. It was a down way from there, on a narrow trail where even a mule would be nervish. And not quiet enough to be an easy trip.

You don't get used to that breed of mountain night noises, not even if you're born and raised there and live and die there. Noises too soft and sneaky to be real whispering voices. Noises like big slow wings, far off and then near. And, above and below the trail, noises like heavy soft paws keeping pace with you, sometimes two paws, sometimes four, sometimes many. They stay with you, such noises as that, all the hours you grope the night trail, all the way down to the valley so low, till you're ready to bless God for the little bitty crumb of light that means a human home, and you ache and pray to get to that home, be it ever so humble, so you can be safe inside with the light.

It's wondered me since if Mr. Yandro's constant chatter was a string of curses or, for maybe the first time in his proud life, a string of prayers.

The light we saw was a pine-knot fire inside a little cabin above the stream that giggled along the valley bottom. The door was open and somebody sat on the stoop.

"Is that a desrick?" panted and puffed Mr. Yandro.

"No, sir, it's newer made. Yonder's Miss Tully at the door, sitting up to think."

Miss Tully recollected me and welcomed us. She was eighty or ninety, without ary tooth in her mouth to clamp her stone-bowl pipe, but she stood straight as a pine on the split-slab floor, and the firelight showed no gray to her neatly combed black hair. "Rest your hats," she bade us. "So this here stranger man is named

Yandro. Funny, sir, you coming just now. You looking for the desrick on Yandro? It's right where it's been," and she pointed with her pipe stem off across the valley and up the far side.

She gave us two chairs bottomed with juniper bark by the fire, and sat on a stool next the shelf with herbs in pots and one-two old paper books, *The Long Lost Friend* and *Egyptian Secrets*, and *Big Albert*, the one they tell you can't be flung away or given away or burnt, only to be got rid of by burying with a funeral prayer, like a human corpse.

"Funny," she said again, not laughing, "you coming along just as the seventy-five years run out."

We inquired her, and she told us what we'd come to hear:

"I was just a pigtail girl back then, when Joris Yandro courted Polly Wiltse, the witch girl. Mr. Yandro, you favor your grandsire a right much. He wasn't nowhere as stout-built as you, and younger by years when last I saw him, though."

Though I'd heard it all before. I harked at it. It was like a many such tale at the start. Polly Wiltse was sure enough a witch, not just a study-witch like Miss Tully, and Polly Wiltse's beauty would melt the heart of nature and make a dumb man cry out, "Praise God Who made her!" But none dared court her save only Joris Yandro, who was handsome for a man as she was lovely for a woman. For it was his wish to get her to show him the gold on top of the mountain named for his folks, that only Polly Wiltse and her witchings could find.

"Sure enough there's gold in these mountains," I answered Mr. Yandro's interrupting question. "The history books tell that before even the California rush, folks mined and minted gold in these parts."

"Gold," he repeated me, both respectful and greedy. "I was right to come."

Miss Tully told that Joris Yandro coaxed Polly

Wiltse to fetch down gold to him, and he carried it off and never came back. And Polly Wiltse pined and mourned like a sick bird, and on Yandro's top she built her desrick. She sang the song, the one I'd sung, it was part of a long charm-spell. Three quarters of a century would pass, seventy-five years, and her love would come back.

"But he didn't," said Mr. Yandro. "My grandfather died up North."

"He sent his grand-boy, who favors him," Miss Tully thumbed tobacco into her pipe. "All the Yandros moved out, purely scared of Polly Wiltse's singing. But the song fetched you back here, just at the right time, to where maybe she's waiting."

"In her desrick, where the wild beasts can't reach her," Mr. Yandro quoted, and laughed. "John says they have bears and wildcats up here." He expected her to say I was wrong.

"Other things, too. Scarced-out animals like the Toller."

"The Toller?" he said.

"The hugest flying thing there is, I reckon," said Miss Tully. "It tolls its voice like a bell, to tell other creatures their feed is come near. And there's the Flat. It lies level with the ground and not much higher, and it can wrop you like a blanket." She lighted the pipe with a splinter from the fire. "And the Bammat. Big, the Bammat is."

"You mean the Behemoth," he suggested.

"No, the Behemoth was in Bible times. The Bammat's hairy-like, with big ears and a long wiggly snaky nose and twisty white teeth sticking out its mouth."

"Oh!" and Mr. Yandro trumpeted his laugh. "You've heard some story about the Mammoth. Why, it's been extinct for thousands of years."

"Not for such a long time, I hear tell," she said, puffing.

"Anyway," he argued on, "the Mammoth, the Bammat as you call it, was of the elephant family. How would it get up in these mountains?"

"Maybe folks hunted it up here," said Miss Tully, "and maybe it stays here so folks'll reckon it's dead and gone these thousand years. Then there's the Behinder."

"And what," inquired Mr. Yandro, "might the Behinder look like?"

"Can't rightly say. For it's always behind the one it's a-fixing to grab. And there's the Skim, it kites through the air. And the Culverin, that can shoot pebbles with its mouth."

"And you believe all that?" sneered Mr. Yandro, the way he always sneered at everything, everywhere.

"Why else do I tell it? Well, sir, you're back where your kin used to live, in the valley where the mountain was named for them. I can let youins sleep here on my front stoop this night."

"I came to climb the mountain and see the desrick" said Mr. Yandro with that anxious hurry to him I kept wondering on.

"You can't climb there till it's light," she said, and she made us up two quilt pallets on the stoop.

I was tired, glad to stretch out, but Mr. Yandro fussed, as if it was wasting time. At sunup, Miss Tully fried us some side meat and some slices of cold-set hominy grits and fixed us a snack to carry, and a gourd for water. Mr. Yandro held out a ten-dollar bill.

"No, I thank you," said Miss Tully. "I bade you stay. I don't take money for such as that."

"Oh, everybody takes money from me," he snickered, and flung it on the door sill at her feet. "Go on, it's yours."

Quick as a weasel, her hand grabbed a big stick of stove wood. "Stoop down and take that money bill back, Mr. Yandro," she said.

He did as she said to do. She pointed the stick out across the stream in the thickets below, and up the height beyond. She acted as if there'd been no trouble a second before.

"That's Yandro Mountain," she said, "and up at the top, where it looks like the crown of a hat, thick with trees all the way up, stands the desrick by Polly Wiltse. Look close with the sun rising, and you can maybe make it out."

I looked hard. There for sure it was, far off and high up. It looked a lean sort of building. "How about trails up?" I asked.

"There's trails up, John, but nobody walks them."

"Now, now," said Mr. Yandro. "If there's a trail, somebody walks it."

"Maybe, but I don't know ary soul in this here valley would set foot to such a trail, not with what they say's up there."

He laughed, as I wouldn't have dared. "You mean the Bammat," he said. "And the Flat and the Skim and the Culverin."

"And the Toller," she added for him, "and the Behinder. Only a gone gump would climb up yonder."

We headed down to the waterside, and crossed on a log. On the far bank led a trail along, and when the sun was an hour up we were at the foot of Yandro's hill and a trail went up there too.

We rested. He needed rest worse than I did. Moving most of the night before, unused to walking and climbing, he had a gaunted look to his heavy face and his clothes were sweated and dust dulled out his shiny shoes. But he grinned at me.

"So she's waited seventy-five years," he said, "and so I look like the man she's waiting for, and so there's gold up there. Gold my grandfather didn't carry off."

"You truly believe what you heard," I said, surprised.

"John, a wise man knows when to believe the unusual, and know how it will profit him. She's waiting up there, and so is the gold."

"What when you find it?" I inquired him.

"My grandfather went off and left her. Sounds like a good example to me." He grinned toothier. "I'll give you some of the gold."

"No, I thank you, Mr. Yandro."

"You don't want pay? Why did you come here with me?"

"Just made up my mind in a moment, like you."

He scowled up the height. "How long will it take to climb?"

"Depends on how fast we keep the pace."

"Let's go," and he started up.

Folks' feet hadn't worn that trail. We saw a hoof mark.

"Deer," grunted Mr. Yandro, and I said, "Maybe."

We scrambled up a rightward slant, then leftward. The trees marched in close with us and their branches filtered just a soft green light. Something rustled. A brown furry shape, bigger than a big cat, scuttled out of sight.

"Woodchuck," wheezed Mr. Yandro, and again I said, "Maybe."

After working up for an hour we rested, and after two hours more we rested again. Around 10 o'clock we got to an open space with clear light, and sat on a log to eat the corn bread and smoked meat Miss Tully had fixed. Mr. Yandro mopped his face with a fancy handkerchief and gobbled food and glittered his eye at me.

"What are you glooming about?" he said. "You look as if you'd call me a name if you weren't afraid to."

"I've held my tongue by way of manners, not fear," I said. "I'm just thinking how and why we came so far and sudden to this place."

"I heard that song you sang and thought I'd see where my people originated. Now I've a hunch about profit. That's enough for you."

"You're more than rich enough without that gold," I said.

"I'm going up," said Mr. Yandro, "because, by God, that old hag down there said everyone's afraid to. And you said you'd go with me."

"Right to the top with you," I promised.

I forebore to say that something was looking from among the trees right behind him. It was big and broad-headed, with elephant ears, and white tusks like banisters on a spiral staircase, but it was woolly-shaggy, like a buffalo bull. How could a thing as big as the Bammat move without making noise?

Mr. Yandro drank from his whiskey bottle, and on we climbed. We heard noises from the woods and brush, behind rocks and down little draws, as if the mountain side thronged with live things, thick as fleas on a possum dog and another sight sneakier.

"Why are you singing under your breath?" he grunted.

"I'm not singing. I need my wind for climbing."

"But I hear it." We stopped on the trail, and I heard it too.

Soft, almost like a half-remembered song in your mind, it was the Yandro song, all right:

"Look away, look away, look away over Yandro
  Where them wild things are a-flyin',
  From bough to bough, and a-mating with their mates,
  So why not me with mine? . . ."

"It comes from above us," I said.

"Then we must be nearly at the top."

As we started to climb again, I heard the noises to right and left, and realized they'd gone quiet when we stopped. They moved when we moved, they waited when we waited. Soft noises, but lots of them.

Which is why I, and Mr. Yandro probably, didn't pause any more on the way up, even on a rocky stretch where we had to climb on all fours. It was about an hour before noon when we got to the top.

There was a circle-shaped clearing, with trees

thronged all the way round except toward the slope. Those trees had mist among and betwixt them, quiet and fluffy, like spider webbing. And at the open space, on the lip of the way down, perched the desrick.

Old-aged was how it looked. It stood high and looked higher, because it was so narrow built of unnotched logs, four set above four, hogpen fashion, tall as a tall tobacco barn. Betwixt the logs was clinking, big masses and wads of clay. The steep roof was of long-cut, narrow shingles, and there was one big door of one axe-chopped plank, with hinges inside, for I saw none. And one window, covered with what must have been rawhide scraped thin, with a glow of soft light soaking through.

"That's the desrick," puffed Mr. Yandro.

Looking at him then, I know what most he wanted on this earth. To be boss. Money just greatened him. His greatness was bigness. He wanted to do all the talking and have everybody else do all the listening. He licked his lips, like a cat over a dish of cream.

"Let's go in," he said.

"Not where I'm not invited," I told him, flat. "I said I'd come with you to the top, and I've done that."

"Come with me. My name's Yandro, and this mountain's name is Yandro. I can buy and sell every man, woman and child in this part of the country. If I say it's all right to go in, it's all right."

He meant that thing. The world and all in it was just there to let him walk on it. He took a step toward the desrick. Somebody hummed inside, not the words of the song, just the tune. Mr. Yandro snorted at me, to show how small he reckoned me to hold back, and headed toward the big door.

"She's going to show me the gold," he said.

Where I stood at the clearing's edge, I was aware of a sort of closing in round the edge, among the trees and brush. Not that it could be seen, but there was a *gong-gong* somewhere, the voice of the Toller saying to the other creatures their feed was near. Above

THE DESRICK ON YANDRO

the treetops sailed a round flat thing like a big plate being flung high. A Skim. Then another Skim. And the blood in my body was as solid cold as ice, and for voice I had a handful of sand in my throat.

Plain as paint I knew that if I tried to back up, to turn round even, my legs would fail and I'd fall down. With fingers like sleety twigs I dragged forward my guitar to touch the silver strings, for silver is protection against evil.

But I never did. For out of some bushes near me the Bammat stuck its broad woolly head and shook it at me once, for silence. It looked me betwixt the eyes, steadier than a beast should ought to look at a man, and shook its head again. I wasn't to make any noise, and I didn't. Then the Bammat paid me no more mind, and I saw I wasn't to be included in what would happen then.

Mr. Yandro knocked at the big plank door. He waited, and knocked again. I heard him rough out that he wasn't used to waiting for his knock to be answered.

The humming had died inside. Mr. Yandro moved around to the window and picked at that rawhide.

I saw, but he couldn't, how around from back of the desrick flowed something. It lay on the ground like a broad, black, short-furred carpet rug. It humped and then flattened, the way a measuring worm moves. It came up pretty fast behind Mr. Yandro. The Toller said *gong-gong-gong,* from closer to us.

"Anybody home?" bawled Mr. Yandro. "Let me in!"

That crawling carpet brushed its edge on his foot. He looked down at it, and his eyes stuck out like two doorknobs. He knew what it was, he named it at the top of his voice.

"The Flat!"

Humping against him, it tried to wrap round his foot and leg. He gobbled out something I'd never want written down for my last words, and pulled loose and ran toward the edge of the clearing.

Gong-gong, said the Toller, and just in front of Mr.

Yandro the Culverin slid into sight on its many legs. It pointed its needly mouth and spit a pebble. I heard the pebble ring on Mr. Yandro's head. He staggered and half fell. And I saw what nobody's ever supposed to see.

The Behinder flung itself on his shoulders. Then I knew why nobody's supposed to see one. I wish I hadn't. To this day I can see it, plain as a fence at noon, and forever I'll be able to see it. But telling about it is another matter. Thank you, gentlemen, I won't try.

Everything else was out—the Bammat, the Culverin, all the others—hustling Mr. Yandro across toward the desrick, and the door moved slowly and quietly open to let him in.

As for me, I hoped and prayed they won't mind if I just went down the trail as fast as I could put one foot below the other.

Scrambling down, without a noise to keep me company, I reckoned I'd probably had my unguessed part in the whole thing. Seventy-five years had to pass, and then Mr. Yandro return to the desrick. It needed me, or somebody like me, to put it in his head and heart to come to where his grandsire had courted Polly Wiltse, just as though it was his own whim.

I told myself this would be a good time to go searching for another valley, a valley where there was a song I wanted to hear and learn, a right pretty song named *Vandy, Vandy*. But meanwhile—

No. No, of course Mr. Yandro wasn't the one who'd made Polly Wiltse love him and then had left her. But he was the man's grand-boy, of the same blood and the same common, low-down, sorry nature that wanted the power of money and never cared who was hurt so he could have his wish. And he looked enough like Joris Yandro so that Polly Wiltse would recognize him.

So I headed out of the valley. I was gone by sundown.

I've never studied much about what Polly Wiltse might could be like, welcoming him into her desrick on Yandro, after waiting there inside for three quarters of a hundred years. Anyway, I never heard that he followed me down. Maybe he's been missed by those who knew him. But I'll lay you any amount of money you name that he's not been mourned.

THE STARS DOWN THERE

"I mean it," she said again. "You can't go any farther than this, because here's where the world comes to its end."

She might could have been a few years older than I was, or a few years younger. She was thin, pretty with all that dark hair and those wide-stretched eyes. The evening was cool around us, and the sun's last edge faded, back on the way I'd come.

"The world's round as a ball," and I kicked a rock off the cliff. "It goes on forever."

And I harked for the rock to hit bottom, but it didn't.

"I'm not trying to fool you," she said. "Here's the ending place of the world. Don't step any closer."

"Just making to look down into the valley," I told her. "I see mist down there."

"It's not mist."

And it wasn't. For down there popped out stars in all their faithful beauty, the same way they popped out over our heads. A skyful of stars. No man could say how far down they were.

"I ask your pardon for doubting you," I said. "It's sure enough the ending place of the world. If you jumped off here, you'd fall forever and ever."

"Forever and ever," she repeated me. "That's what I think. That's what I hope. That's why I came out here this evening."

Before I could grab hold of her, she'd jumped. Stooping, I watched her falling, littler and littler against the stars down there, till at last I could see her no more.

VANDY, VANDY

Nary name that valley had. Such outside folks as knew about it just said, "Back in yonder," and folks inside said, "Here." The mail truck would drop a few letters in a hollow tree next to a ridge where the trail went up and over and down. Three-four times a year bearded men in homemade clothes and shoes fetched out their makings—clay dishes and pots, mostly—for dealers to sell to the touristers. They toted back coffee, salt, gunpowder, a few nails. Stuff like that.

It was a day's scramble along that ridge trail. I vow, even with my long legs and no load but my silver-strung guitar. The thick, big old trees had never been cut, for lumber nor yet for cleared land. I found a stream, quenched my thirst, and followed it down. Near sunset time, I heard music a-jangling, and headed for that.

Fire shone out through an open cabin door, to where folks sat on a stoop log and front-yard rocks. One had a banjo, another fiddled, and the rest slapped hands so a boy about ten or twelve could jig. Then they spied me and fell quiet. They looked at me, but they didn't know me.

"That was right pretty, ladies and gentlemen," I said, walking in, but nobody remarked.

A long-bearded old man with one suspender and no shoes held the fiddle on his knee. I reckoned he was the grandsire. A younger, shorter-bearded man with the banjo might could be his son. There was a dry old mother, there was the son's plump wife, there was a young yellow-haired girl, and there was that dancing little grandboy.

"What can we do for you, young sir?" the old man asked. Not that he sounded like doing aught—mountain folks say that even to the government man who comes hunting a still on their place.

"Why," I said, "I sort of want a place to sleep."

"Right much land to stretch out on down the hollow a piece," said the banjo man.

I tried again. "I was hearing you folks play first part of *Fire in the Mountains*."

"Is they two parts?" That was the boy, before anyone could silence him.

"Sure enough, son," I said. "I'll play you the second part."

The old man opened his beard, like enough to say wait till I was asked, but I strummed my guitar into second part, best I knew how. Then I played the first part through, and, "You sure God can pick that," said the short-bearded one. "Do it again."

I did it again. When I reached the second part, the fiddle and banjo joined me in. We went round *Fire in the Mountains* one time more, and the lady-folks clapped hands and the boy jigged. When we stopped, the old man made me a nod.

"Sit on that there rock," he said. "What might we call you?"

"My name's John."

"I'm Tewk Millen. Mother, I reckon John's a-tired, coming from outside. Might be he'd relish a gourd of cold water."

"We're just before having a bite," the old lady said to me. "Ain't but just smoke meat and beans, but you're welcome."

"I'm sure enough honored, Mrs. Millen," I said. "But I don't wish to be a trouble to you."

"No trouble," said Mr. Tewk Millen. "Let me make you known to my son Heber and his wife Jill, and this here is their boy Calder."

"Proud to know you, John," they said.

"And my girl Vandy," said Mr. Tewk.

I looked on her hair like yellow corn silk and her eyes like purple violets. "Miss Vandy," I said.

Shy, she dimpled at me. "I know that's a scarce name, Mr. John. I never heard it anywhere but among my kinfolks."

"I have," I said. "It's what brought me here."

Mr. Tewk Millen looked funny above his whiskers. "Thought you was a young stranger-man."

"I heard the name outside, in a song, sir. Somebody allowed the song's known here. I'm a singer, I go a far piece after a good song." I looked around. "Do you folks know that Vandy song?"

"Yes, sir," said little Calder, but the others studied a minute. Mr. Tewk rubbed up a leaf of tobacco into his pipe.

"Calder," he said, "go in and fetch me a chunk of fire to light up with. John, you certain sure you never met my girl Vandy?"

"Sure as can be," I replied him. "Only I can figure how any young fellow might come long miles to meet her."

She stared down at her hands in her lap. "We learnt the song from papa," she half-whispered, "and he learnt it from his papa."

"And my papa learnt it from his," finished Mr. Tewk for her. "I reckon that song goes long years back."

"I'd relish hearing it," I said.

"After you learnt it yourself," said Mr. Tewk, "what would you do then?"

"Go back outside," I said, "and sing it some."

He enjoyed to hear me say that. "Heber," he told his son, "you pick out and I'll scrape this fiddle, and Calder and Vandy can sing it for John."

They played the tune through once without words. The notes came together lonesomely, in what schooled folks call minors. But other folks, better schooled yet, say such tunes come out strange and lonesome because in the ancient times folks had another note-scale from our do-re-mi-fa today. Little Calder piped up, high and young but strong:

"Vandy, Vandy, I've come to court you,
Be you rich or be you poor,
And if you'll kindly entertain me,
I will love you forever more.

"Vandy, Vandy, I've gold and silver,
Vandy, Vandy, I've a house and land,
Vandy, Vandy, I've a world of pleasure,
I would make you a handsome man. . . ."

He sang that far for the fellow come courting, and Vandy sang back the reply, sweet as a bird:

"I love a man who's in the army,
He's been there for seven long years,
And if he's there for seven years longer,
I won't court no other dear.

"What care I for your gold and silver,
What care I for—"

She stopped, and the fiddle and banjo stopped, and it was like the sudden death of sound. The leaves didn't rustle in the trees, nor the fire didn't stir on the hearth inside. They all looked with their mouths half open, where somebody stood with his hands crossed on the gold knob of a black cane and grinned all on one side of his toothy mouth.

Maybe he'd come down the stream trail, maybe he'd dropped from a tree like a possum. He was built slim and spry, with a long coat buttoned to his pointed chin, and brown pants tucked into elastic-sided boots, like what your grand-sire wore. His hands on the cane looked slim and strong. His face, bar its crooked smile, might could be called handsome. His dark brown hair curled like buffalo wool, and his eyes were as shiny pale gray as a new knife. Their gaze crawled all over us, and he laughed a slow, soft laugh.

"I thought I'd stop by," he crooned out, "if I haven't worn out my welcome."

"Oh, *no*, sir!" said Mr. Tewk, quick standing up on his two bare feet, fiddle in hand. "No, sir, Mr. Loden, we're right proud to have you," he jabber-squawked, like a rooster caught by the leg. "You sit down, sir, make yourself easy."

Mr. Loden sat down on the rock Mr. Tewk had got up from, and Mr. Tewk found a place on the stoop log by his wife, nervous as a boy caught stealing apples.

"Your servant, Mrs. Millen," said Mr. Loden. "Heber, you look well, and your good wife. Calder, I brought you candy."

His slim hand offered a bright striped stick, red and yellow. You'd think a country child would snatch it. But Calder took it slow and scared, as he'd take a poison snake. You'd know he'd decline if only he dared, but he didn't dare.

"For you, Mr. Tewk," went on Mr. Loden, "I fetched some of my tobacco, an excellent weed." He handed out a soft brown leather pouch. "Empty your pipe and fill it with this."

"Thank you kindly," said Mr. Tewk, and sighed, and began to do as he'd been ordered.

"Miss Vandy." Mr. Loden's crooning voice petted her name. "I wouldn't venture here without hoping you'd receive a trifle at my hands."

He dangled it from a chain, a gold thing the size of his pink thumbnail. In it shone a white jewel that grabbed the firelight and twinkled red.

"Do me the honor, Miss Vandy, to let it rest on your heart, that I may envy it."

She took the thing and sat with it between her soft

little hands. Mr. Loden's eye-knives turned on me.

"Now," he said, "we come round to the stranger within your gates."

"We come around to me," I agreed him, hugging my guitar on my knees. "My name's John, sir."

"Where are you from, John?" It was sudden, almost fierce, like a lawyer in court.

"From nowhere," I said.

"Meaning, from everywhere," he supplied me. "What do you do?"

"I wander," I said. "I sing songs. I mind my business and watch my manners."

"*Touché!*" he cried out in a foreign tongue, and smiled on that one side of his mouth. "My duties and apologies, John, if my country ways seem rude to a world traveler. No offense meant."

"None taken," I said, and didn't add that country ways are most times polite ways.

"Mr. Loden," put in Mr. Tewk again, "I make bold to offer you what poor rations my old woman's made for us—"

"They're good enough for the best man living," Mr. Loden broke him off. "I'll help Mrs. Millen prepare them. After you, ma'am."

She walked in, and he followed. What he said there was what happened.

"Miss Vandy," he said over his shoulder, "you might help."

She went in, too. Dishes clattered. Through the doorway I saw Mr. Loden fling a tweak of powder in the skillet. The menfolks sat outside and said naught. They might have been nailed down, with stones in their mouths. I studied what might could make a proud, honorable mountain family so scared of a guest, and knew it wouldn't be a natural thing. It would be a thing beyond nature or the world.

Finally little Calder said, "Maybe we'll finish the singing after while," and his voice was a weak young voice now.

"I recollect another song from around here," I said. "About the fair and blooming wife."

Those closed mouths all snapped open, then shut again. Touching the silver strings, I began:

> "There was a fair and blooming wife
> And of children she had three,
> She sent them to a Northern school
> To study gramarie.
>
> "But the King's men came upon that school,
> And when sword and rope had done,
> Of the children three she sent away,
> Returned to her but one. . . ."

"Supper's made," said Mrs. Millen from inside.

We went in to where there was a trestle table and a clean home-woven cloth and clay dishes set out. Mr. Loden, by the pots at the fire, waved for Mrs. Millen and Vandy to dish up the food.

It wasn't smoke meat and beans I saw on my plate. Whatever it might be, it wasn't that. They all looked at their helps of food, but not even Calder took any till Mr. Loden sat down.

"Why," said Mr. Loden, "one would think you feared poison."

Then Mr. Tewk forked up a bit and put it into his beard. Calder did likewise, and the others. I took a mouthful; sure enough, it tasted good.

"Let me honor your cooking, sir," I told Mr. Loden. "It's like witch magic."

His eyes came on me, and he laughed, short and sharp.

"John, you were singing about the blooming wife," he said. "She had three children who went North to study gramarie. Do you know what gramarie means?"

"Grammar," spoke up Calder. "The right way to talk."

"Hush," whispered his father, and he hushed.

"Why," I replied. "Mr. Loden, I've heard that gramarie is witch stuff, witch knowledge and power. That Northern school could have been at only one place."

"What place, John?" he almost sang under his breath.

"A Massachusetts Yankee town called Salem. Around three hundred years back—"

"Not by so much," said Mr. Loden. "In 1692, John."

Everybody was staring above those steaming plates.

"A preacher-man named Cotton Mather found them teaching the witch stuff to children," I said. "I hear tell they killed twenty folks, mostly the wrong ones, but two-three were sure enough witches."

"George Burroughs," said Mr. Loden, half to himself. "Martha Carrier. And Bridget Bishop. They were real. But others got safe away, and one young child of the three. Somebody owed that child the two young lost lives of his brothers, John."

"I call something else to mind," I said. "They scare young folks with the tale. The one child lived to be a hundred, and his son likewise and a hundred years of life, and his son's son a hundred more. Maybe that's why I thought the witch school at Salem was three hundred years back."

"Not by so much, John," he said again. "Even give that child that got away the age of Calder there, it would be only about two hundred and eighty years, or thereabouts."

He was daring any of Mr. Tewk Millen's family to speak or even breathe heavy, and none took the dare.

"From three hundred, that would leave twenty," I reckoned. "A lot can be done in twenty years, Mr. Loden."

"That's the naked truth," he said, the knives of his eyes on Vandy's young face, and he got up and bowed all round. "I thank you all for your hospitality. I'll come again if I may."

"Yes, sir," said Mr. Tewk in a hurry, but Mr. Loden looked at Vandy and waited.

"Yes, sir," she told him, as if it would choke her.

He took his gold-headed cane, and gazed a hard gaze at me. Then I did a rude thing, but it was all I could think of.

"I don't feel right, Mrs. Millen, not paying for what you gave me," I allowed, getting up myself. From my dungaree pocket I took a silver quarter and dropped it on the table, right in front of Mr. Loden.

"Take it away!" he squeaked, high as a bat, and out of the house he was gone, bat-quick and bat-sudden.

The others gopped after him. Outside the night had fallen, thick as black wool round the cabin. Mr. Tewk cleared his throat.

"John, I hope you're better raised than that," he said. "We don't take money from nobody we bid to our table. Pick it up."

"Yes, sir, I ask pardon."

Putting away the quarter, I felt a mite better. I'd done that one other time with a silver quarter, I'd scared Mr. Onselm almost out of the black art. So Mr. Loden was a witch man, too, and could be scared the same way. I reckon I was foolish for the lack of sense to think it would be as easy as that.

I walked outside, leaving Mrs. Millen and Vandy to do the dishes. The firelight showed me the stoop log to sit on. I touched my guitar strings and began to pick out the *Vandy, Vandy* tune, soft and gentle. After while, Calder came out and sat beside me and sang the words. I liked best the last verse:

"Wake up, wake up! The dawn is breaking.
Wake up, wake up! It's almost day.
Open up your doors and your divers windows,
See my true love march away. . . ."

"Mr. John," said Calder, "I never made sure what divers windows is."

"That's an old-timey word," I said. "It means different kinds of windows. Another thing proves it's a right old song. A man seven years in the army must have gone to the first war with the English. It lasted longer here in the South than other places—from 1775 to 1782. How old are you, Calder?"

"Rising onto ten."

"Big for your age. A boy your years in 1692 would be a hundred if he lived to 1782, when the English war was near done and somebody or other had been seven years in the army."

"Washington's army," said Calder. "King Washington."

"King who?" I asked.

"Mr. Loden calls him King Washington—the man that hell-drove the English soldiers and rules in his own name town."

So that's what they thought in that valley. I never said that Washington was no king but a president, and that he'd died and gone to his rest when his work was done and his country safe. I kept thinking about somebody a hundred years old in 1782, trying to court a girl whose true love was seven years marched off in the army.

"Calder," I said, "does the *Vandy, Vandy* song tell about your own folks?"

He looked into the cabin. Nobody listened. I struck a chord on the silver strings. He said, "I've heard tell so, Mr. John."

I hushed the strings with my hand, and he talked on:

"I reckon you've heard some about it. That witch child that lived to be a hundred—he come courting a girl named Vandy, but she was a good girl."

"Bad folks sometimes try to court good ones," I said.

"She wouldn't have him, not with all his land and money. And when he pressed her, her soldier man come home, and in his hand was his discharge-writing, and on it King Washington's name. He was free from the war. He was Hosea Tewk, my grandsire some few times removed. And my own grandsire's mother was Vandy Tewk, and my sister is Vandy Millen."

"What about the hundred-year-old witch man?"

Calder looked round again. Then he said, "I reckon he got him some other girl to birth him a son, and we think that son married at another hundred years, and his son is Mr. Loden, the grandson of the first witch man."

"Your grandsire's mother, Vandy Tewk—how old would she be, Calder?"

"She's dead and gone, but she was born the first year her pa was off fighting the Yankees."

Eighteen sixty-one, then. In 1882, end of the second hundred years, she'd have been ripe for courting. "And she married a Millen," I said.

"Yes, sir. Even when the Mr. Loden that lived then tried to court her. But she married Mr. Washington Millen. That was my great-grandsire. He wasn't feared of aught. He was like King Washington."

I picked a silver string. "No witch man got the first Vandy," I reminded him. "Nor yet the second Vandy."

"A witch man wants the Vandy that's here now," said Calder. "Mr. John, I wish you'd steal her away from him."

I got up. "Tell your folks I've gone for a night walk."

"Not to Mr. Loden's." His face was pale beside me. "He won't let you come."

The night was more than black then, it was solid. No sound in it. No life. I won't say I couldn't have stepped off into it, but I didn't. I sat down again. Mr. Tewk spoke my name, then Vandy.

We sat in front of the cabin and spoke about weather and crops. Vandy was at my one side, Calder at the other. We sang—*Dream True,* I recollect, and *The Rebel Soldier.* Vandy sang the sweetest I'd ever heard, but while I played I felt that somebody harked in the blackness. If it was on Yandro Mountain and not in the valley, I'd have feared the Behinder sneaking close, or the Flat under our feet. But Vandy's violet eyes looked happy at me, her rose lips smiled.

Finally Vandy and Mrs. Millen said good night and went into a back room. Heber and his wife and Calder laddered up into the loft. Mr. Tewk offered to make me a pallet bed by the fire.

"I'll sleep at the door," I told him.

He looked at me, at the door. And: "Have it your way," he said.

I pulled off my shoes. I said a prayer and stretched out on the quilt he gave me. But long after the others must have been sleeping, I lay and listened.

Hours afterward, the sound came. The fire was just only a coal ember, red light was soft in the cabin when I heard the snicker. Mr. Loden stooped over me at the door sill.

"I won't let you come in," I said to him.

"Oh, you're awake," he said. "The others are asleep, by my doing. And you can't move, any more than they can."

It was true. I couldn't sit up. I might have been dried into clay, like a frog or a lizard that must wait for the rain.

"Bind," he said above me. "Bind, bind. Unless you can count the stars or the ocean drops, be bound."

It was a spell saying. "From the *Long-Lost Friend?*" I asked.

"Albertus Magnus. The book they say he wrote."

"I've seen the book."

"You'll lie where you are till sunrise. Then—"

I tried to get up. It was no use.

"See this?" He held it to my face. It was my picture, drawn true to how I looked. He had the drawing gift. "At sunrise I'll strike it with this."

He laid the picture on the ground. Then he brought forward his gold-headed cane. He twisted the handle, and out of the cane's inside he drew a blade of pale iron, thin and mean as a snake. There was writing on it, but I couldn't read in that darkness.

"I'll touch my point to your picture," he said. "Then you'll bother Vandy and me no more. I should have done that to Hosea Tewk."

"Hosea Tewk," I said after him, "or Washington Millen."

The tip of his blade stirred in front of my eyes. "Don't say that name, John."

"Washington Millen," I said it again. "Named for George Washington. Did you hate Washington when you knew him?"

He took a long, mean breath, as if cold rain fell on him. "You've guessed what these folks haven't guessed, John."

"I've guessed you're not a witch man's grandson, but a witch woman's son," I said. "You got free from that Salem school in 1692. You've lived near three hundred years, and when they're over, you know where you'll go and burn, forever amen."

His blade hung over my throat, like a wasp over a ripe peach. Then he drew it back. "No," he told himself. "The Millens would know I'd stabbed you. Let them think you died in your sleep."

"You knew Washington," I said again. "Maybe—"

"Maybe I offered him help, and he was foolish enough to refuse it. Maybe—"

"Maybe Washington scared you off from him," I broke in the way he had, "and won his war without your witch magic. And maybe that was bad for you, because the one who'd given you three hundred years expected pay—good hearts turned into bad ones. Then you tried to win Vandy for yourself, the first Vandy."

"A little for myself," he half sang, "but mostly for—"

"Mostly for who gave you three hundred years," I finished for him.

I was tightening and swelling my muscles, trying to

pull a-loose from what held me down. I might as well have tried to wear my way through solid rock.

"Vandy," Mr. Loden's voice touched her name. "The third Vandy, the sweeeest and the best. She's like a spring day and like a summer night. When I see her with a bucket at the spring or a basket in the garden, my eyes swim, John. It's as if I see a spirit walking past."

"A good spirit," I said. "Your time's short. You want to win her from good ways to bad ways."

"Her voice is like a lark's," he crooned, the blade low in his hand. "It's like wind over a bank of roses and violets. It's like the light of stars turned into music."

"And you want to lead her down into hell," I said.

"Maybe we won't go to hell, or to heaven either. Maybe we'll live and live. Why don't you say something about that, John?"

"I'm thinking," I made answer, and I was. I was trying to remember what I had to remember.

It's in the third part of the Albertus Magnus book Mr. Loden had mentioned, the third part full of holy names he sure enough would never read. I'd seen it, as I'd told him. If the words would come back to me—

Something sent part of them.

"The cross in my right hand," I said, too soft for him to hear, "that I may travel the open land. . . ."

"Maybe three hundred years more," said Mr. Loden, "without anyone like Hosea Tewk, or Washington Millen, or you, John, to stop us. Three hundred years with Vandy, and she'll know the things I know, do the things I do."

I'd been able to twist my right forefinger over my middle one, for the cross in my right hand. I said more words as I remembered:

". . . So must I be loosed and blessed, as the cup and the holy bread. . . ."

Now my left hand could creep along my side, as far as my belt. But it couldn't lift up just yet, because I couldn't think of the rest of the charm.

"The night's black just before dawn," Mr. Loden was saying. "I'll make my fire. When I've done what I'll do, I can step over your dead body, and Vandy's mine."

"Don't you fear Washington?" I asked him, and my left fingertips were in my dungaree pocket.

"Can he come from the place to which he's gone? Washington has forgotten me and our old falling-out."

"Where he is, he remembers you," I said.

Mr. Loden was on his knee. His blade point scratched a circle round him on the ground. The circle held him and the paper with my picture. Then he took a sack from inside his coat, and poured powder along the scratched circle. He stood up, and golden-brown fire jumped up around him.

"Now we begin," he said.

He sketched in the air with his blade. He put his boot toe on my picture. He looked into the golden-brown fire.

"I made my wish before this," he spaced out the words. "I make it now. There was no day when I have not seen my wish fulfilled."

Paler than the fire shone his eyes.

"No son to follow John. No daughter to mourn him."

My fingers in my pocket touched something round and thin. The quarter he'd been scared by, that Mr. Tewk Millen had made me take back.

Mr. Loden spoke names I didn't like to hear. "Haade," he said. "Mikaded. Rakeben. Rika. Tasarith. Modeka."

My hand worried out, and in it the quarter.

"Truth," said Mr. Loden. "Tumch. Here with this image I slay—"

I lifted my left hand three inches and flung the quarter. My heart went rotten with sick sorrow, for it didn't hit Mr. Loden—it fell into the fire—

Then in one place up there shot white smoke, like a steam puff from an engine, and the fire died down everywhere else. Mr. Loden stopped his spell-speaking and wavered back. I saw the glow of his goggling eyes and of his open mouth.

Where the steamy smoke had puffed, it was making a shape.

Taller than a man. Taller than Mr. Loden or me. Wide-shouldered, long-legged, with a dark tail coat and high boots and hair tied back behind the head. It turned, and I saw the brave face, the big, big nose—

"King Washington!" screamed out Mr. Loden, and tried to stab.

But a long hand like a tongs caught his wrist, and I heard the bones break like dry sticks, and Mr. Loden whinnied like a horse that's been bad hurt. That was the grip of the man who'd been America's strongest, who could jump twenty-four feet broad or throw a dollar across the Rappahannock River or wrestle down his biggest soldier.

The other hand came across, flat and stiff, to strike. It sounded like a door a-slamming in a high wind, and Mr. Loden never needed to be struck the second time. His head sagged over widewise. When the grip left his broken wrist, he fell at the booted feet.

I sat up, and stood up. The big nose turned to me, just a second. The head nodded. Friendly. Then it was gone back into steam, into nothing.

I'd said the truth. Where George Washington had been, he'd remembered Mr. Loden. And the silver quarter, with his picture on it, had struck the fire just when Mr. Loden was conjuring with a picture he was making real. And then there had happened what had happened.

A pale streak went up the back sky for the first dawn. There was no fire left, and of the quarter was just a spatter of melted silver. And there was no Mr. Loden, only a mouldy little heap like a rotted-out stump or a hammock or loam or what might could be left of a man that death had caught up with after two hundred years. I picked up the iron blade and broke it on my knee and flung it away into the trees. Then I picked up the paper with my drawn picture. It wasn't hurt a bit, and it looked a right much like me.

Inside the door I put that picture, on the quilt where I'd lain. Maybe the Millens would keep it to remember me by, after they found I was gone and that Mr. Loden came round no more to try to court Vandy. Then I started away, carrying my guitar. If I made good time, I'd be out of the valley by high noon.

As I went, pots started to rattle. Somebody was awake in the cabin. And it was hard, hard, not to turn back when Vandy sang to herself, not thinking what she sang:

"Wake up, wake up! The dawn is breaking.
Wake up, wake up! It's almost day.
Open up your doors and your divers windows,
See my true love march away. . . ."

BLUE MONKEY

'll turn this potful of pebbles into gold," the fat man told us at midnight, "if you all keep from thinking about the blue monkey."

He poured in wine, olive oil, salt. With each he said a certain word. He put on the lid and walked three times round the pot, singing a certain song. But when he tipped the pot over, just pebbles poured out.

"Which of you was thinking about a blue monkey?"

All allowed they'd thought of naught else. Except me—I'd striven to remember exactly what he'd said and done. And all vowed that gold-making joke was a laughing thing.

One midnight a year later and far away I put pebbles in a pot at another doings, and told the folks: "I'll turn them into gold if you all keep from thinking about a red fish."

I poured in the wine, the olive oil, the salt, saying the word that went with each. I covered the pot, walked the three times, sang the song. I asked: "Did anybody think about a blue monkey?"

"But John," said the prettiest lady, "you said not to think about a red fish, and that's what I couldn't put out of my head."

"That was to keep you from thinking about a blue monkey," I said and took up the lid.

Inside the pebbles shone yellow. The prettiest lady picked up two-three. They clinked together in her rosy hand.

"Gold!" she squeaked. "Enough to make you rich, John!"

"Divide it up among you," I said. "Gold's not what I want, nor yet richness."

DUMB SUPPER

Down it rained on hill and hollow, the way you'd think the sky was too worn out to hold it back. It fell so thick and hard that fish could have swum in it, all round where we sat holed up under the country store's low wide porch, five of us. A leather-coated deputy sheriff with a pickup truck; a farmer, who'd put up his mule wagon in a shed behind; the old storekeeper, and us two strangers in that part of the hills, a quiet old gentleman and me with my silver-strung guitar.

As it got dark the storekeeper hung a lantern to a porch rafter. The farmer bought us all a bottle of soda, and the storekeeper busted open a box of cookies. "You'll be here a spell, so sit comfortable," he said. "Friend," he said to me, "did I inquire your name?"

"John," I named myself.

"Well, John, do you play that there guitar, you're a-toting?"

I played and sang for them, that old one about the hunter's true love:

> "Call me darling, call me dear,
> Call me what you will,
> Call me from the valley low,
> Call me from the hill. . . ."

Then we talked about old things and thoughts. I recollect some of what was said, such as:

You can't win solitaire by cheating just once, you've got to keep on cheating; some animals are smarter than folks; who were the Ancients who dug the mineholes in the Toe River county, and what were they seeking, and did they find it; who can say what makes the lights come and go like giant fireflies every night on Brown Mountain; you'll never see a man exactly six feet tall, because that was the height of the Lord Jesus.

The farmer, who next to me was the youngest there, mentioned love and courting, how when you love someone true and need your eyes and thoughts clearest, they mist up and maybe cause you trouble. That led to how you step down a mullein stalk toward your true love's house, and if it grows up again she loves you; and how the girls used to have dumb suppers, setting plates and knives and forks on the table at night and each girl standing behind a chair put ready, and at midnight the candles blew out and a girl thought she saw a ghostly-looking somebody in the chair before her, with the favor of the man she'd marry.

"Knowed of dumb suppers when I was just a chap," allowed the storekeeper, "but most of the old folks then, they never relished the notion. Said it was a devil-made thing, and you might could call in something better left outside."

"Ain't no such goings-on in this day and time," nodded the farmer. "I don't take no stock in them crazy doings."

Back where I was born and raised, in the Drowning Creek country, I'd heard tell of dumb suppers; but I'd never seen one, so I held my tongue. But the deputy grinned his teeth at the farmer.

"You plant by the moon, don't you?" he asked. "Above-ground things like corn at the full, and underground things like taters in the dark?"

"That ain't foolishness, that's the true way," the

farmer said back. "Ask anybody's got a lick of sense about farming."

Then a big wiggling three-forked flash of lightning struck, it didn't seem more than arm-length off, and the thunder was like the falling in of the hills.

"Law me," said the old gentleman, whose name seemed to be Mr. Jay. "That was a hooter."

"It sure God was," the farmer agreed him. "Old Forney Meechum wants us to remember he makes the rain round here."

My ears upped like a rabbit's. "I did hear tell this was the old Meechum-Donovant feud country," I said. "I always wanted to hear the true tale of that. And what about Forney Meechum making the rain—isn't he dead?"

"Deader than hell, John," the storekeeper said. "Though folks never thought he'd die, thought he'd just ugly away. But him and all the Meechum and Donovant men got killed. Both the names died plumb out, I reckon, yonder in the valley so low where you see the rain a-falling the lavishest. I used to hear about it when I was just a chap."

"Me too," nodded the deputy. "Way I got it, Forney Meechum went somewheres west when he was young. Was with the James boys or the Dalton boys, or maybe somebody not quite that respectable."

"And when he come back," took up the storekeeper again, "he could make it rain whenever it suited him."

"How?" I asked, and old Mr. Jay was listening, too.

"Ain't rightly certain how," said the farmer. "I been told he used to mix up mud in a hole, and sing a certain song. Ever hear such a song as that, John?"

I shook my head no, and he went on:

"Forney Meechum done scarier things than that. He witched wells dry. He raised up dead ghosts to show him where treasure was hid. Even his own kinfolks was scared of him, and took orders from him.

So when he fell out with Captain Sam Donovant over a property line, he made all the Meechums break with all the Donovants."

"Fact," said the storekeeper, who wanted to tell the tale his own self. "Then Meechums done what he told them, saving only his cousin's oldest girl, Miss Lute Meechum. And she'd swore eternal love with Captain Donovant's second boy Jeremiah."

Another lightning flash, another thunder growl. Old Mr. Jay hunched his thin shoulders under his jeans coat, and allowed he'd pay for some crackers and cheese if the storekeeper'd fetch them out to us.

"I ain't even now wanting to talk against Forney Meechum," said the farmer. "But they tell he'd put his eye on Lute for himself, and he'd quarrelled with his own son Derwood about who'd have her. But next court day at the county seat, was a fight betwixt Jeremiah Donovant and Derwood Meechum, and Jeremiah put a knife in Derwood and killed him dead."

Mr. Jay leaned forward. The lantern light showed the gray stubble on his gentle old face. "Who drew the first knife?" he asked.

"They say Derwood drew the knife, and Jeremiah took it away and stuck it in him," said the farmer. "Anyway, Jeremiah Donovant had to run from the law, and down in that valley yonder the Meechums and the Donovants began a-shooting at one another."

"Fact," the storekeeper took it up again as he fetched out the crackers and cheese. "That was fifty years back, the last fight of all. Ary man on both sides was killed, down to boys of ten-twelve years. Old Forney called for rain, but somebody shot him just as he got it started."

"And it falls a right much to this day," said the farmer, gazing at the pour from the eaves. "That valley below us is so rainy it's a swamp like. And the widows and orphans that was left alive, both families, they was purely rained out and went other places to live."

"What about Miss Lute Meechum?" I asked next.

"I wondered about her, too," said Mr. Jay.

"Died," said the storekeeper. "Some folks allow it was pure down grief that killed her, that and lonesomeness for that run-off Jeremiah Donovant. I likewise heard tell old Forney shot her when she said for once and all she wouldn't have him."

The deputy sipped his soda. "All done and past now," he said. "Looks like we're rained in here for all night, gentlemen."

But we weren't. It slacked off while we ate our cheese, and then it was just a drip from the branches. The clouds shredded and the moon poked through a moment, shy, like a girl at her first play-party. The deputy got up from the slab bench where he'd been a-sitting.

"Hope my truck'll wallow up that muddy road to town," he said. "Who can I carry with me?"

"I got my mule," added the farmer. "I'll follow along and snake you out when you get stuck in one of them mud holes. John, you and Mr. Jay better ride with me."

I shook my head. "I'm not going to town, thank you kindly. I'm going down that valley trail. Up on the yonder side, I can catch a bus from Sky Notch. I got an errand to do there for a friend."

Mr. Jay said he'd take that trail too. The storekeeper offered to let us sleep in his feed shed, but I said I'd better start. "Coming, sir?" I asked old Mr. Jay.

"After while," he replied me, so I went on alone. Three minutes down trail between those dark wet trees, and the lantern light under the porch was gone as if it hadn't ever shone.

Gentlemen, it was lonesome and dark and wet. I felt my muddy way along, with my brogan shoes all squashy full of water. And yet, sometimes, it wasn't as lonesome as you might call for. There were soft noises, like whispers or crawlings; and once there was a howl, not too far away, like a dog, or either a man trying to sound like a dog, or maybe the neither of them. And it came on to rain again.

I hauled off my old coat to wrap my guitar in it. Not much to see ahead, and I kept on going down slope and down slope, and no way of telling how far down it went before it would start up again to the hills, on the other side where I could catch that bus. I told myself I was a gone gump not to stay at the store, the way I'd been so kindly bid. I hoped that old Mr. Jay had the sense to stay under cover. But it was too far to go back. And I'd better find some place out of the wet, more for my guitar than for me.

Must have been a bend to that trail, because I came all at once in view of the light in the cabin's glass window, before I notioned there was ary living place round there. The light looked warm yellow through the rain, and I hastened my wet muddy feet. Close enough in, I could judge it was an old-made log house, the log-corners notched and locked and the spaces between chinked with clay, and the wide eaves with thick-split shakes on them, but I couldn't really see. "Hello, the house!" I yelled out.

Nary sound back. Maybe the rain kept them from hearing me. I felt my way back to the flat stone at the door, and knocked. No stir inside.

Groping for a knob, I found none, only a leather latch string, old, old style. And, old style, it was out. In my grandsire's day, a latch string out meant come in. I pulled, and a wooden latch lifted inside and the door swung inwards before me.

The room was lit from a fireplace full of red coals, and from a candle stuck on a dish on a table middle-way of the puncheon floor. That table took my eye as I stepped in. A cloth on it, and a plate of old white china with fork and knife at the sides, and a cup and saucer, yes, and a folded napkin. But no food on the table, no coffee in the cup. A chair was set to the plate, and behind the chair, her hands crossed on its back, stood a woman, young and tall and proud to see.

She didn't move. Nothing moved, except the candle flame in the stir of air from the open door. She might could have been cut from wood and put up there to fool folks. I closed the door against the hard drum of the rain, and tracked wet marks on the puncheons as I came toward the table. I took off my old hat, and the water fell from it.

"Good evening, ma'am," I said.

Then her dark eyes moved in her pale face, her sweet firm-jawed face. Her short sad mouth opened, slow and shaky.

"You're not—" she started to mumble, half to herself. "I never meant—"

There was a coppery-looking light moving in her hair as she bent her head and looked down into the empty plate. And then I recollected that talk under the store porch.

"Dumb supper," I said. "I'm right sorry. It was the rain drove me in here. I reckon this is the only house hereabouts, and when nobody answered I just walked in. I didn't mean to pester you."

But I couldn't help myself but look at how she'd set the dumb supper out. Knowing such things weren't done any more, hearing that very thing said that very night, I was wondered to find it. Through my mind kept a-running how some scholar folks say it's a way of doing that came over the Old Country, where dumb suppers were set clear back to time's beginning. Things that old don't die easy after all, I reckoned.

"He'll still come and sit down," she said to me in her soft voice, that was like a low-playing flute heard far off. "I've called him and he'll come."

I hung up my wet coat by the fireplace, and she saw my guitar.

"Sing," she said. "Tole him here to me."

I felt like doing whatever she bade me. I swung the guitar in front of me, and began the song I'd given them at the store:

> "Call me darling, call me dear,
> Call me what you will,
> Call me from the valley low,
> Call me from the hill.
>
> "I hear you as the turtle dove
> That flies from bough to bough,
> And as she softly calls her mate,
> You call me softly now. . . ."

One long hand waved for me to stop, and I stopped with the silver strings still whispering to both of us. I felt my ears close up tight, the way they feel when you've climbed high, high up on a mountain top.

"There's a power working here," I said.

"Yes," she barely made herself heard.

The fire, that had been just coals, found something to blaze up on. Smoke rose dark above the bright flames. The rain outside came barreling down, and there was a wind rising, too, with a whoop and a shove to it that made the locked joints of the cabin's logs creak.

"Sounds like old Forney Meechum's hard at work," I half tried to make a joke, but she didn't take it as such. Her dark-bright eyes lifted their lids to widen, and her hands, on the chair back again, took hold hard.

"Forney doesn't want me to do this," she told me, as if it was my ordinary business.

"He's dead," I reminded her, the way I'd remind a child.

"No," she shook her coppery head. "He's not dead, not all of him. And not all of me, either."

I wondered what she meant, and I stepped away from the fire that was burning bright and hot.

"Are you a Meechum or a Donovant?" I asked.

"A Meechum. But my true love's a Donovant."

"Like Lute Meechum and Jeremiah Donovant?"

"You know about that." Her hands trembled a mite, for all they held to the chair so hard. "Who are you?"

"My name's John." I touched the silver strings to make them whisper again. "Yes, I know the tale of that feud. Forney Meechum, who could witch down the rain, said Jeremiah mustn't have Lute—"

"He's here!" she cried out, with her voice loud at last.

The wind shook the cabin like a dice-box. The shakes on the roof must have ruffed up like a hen's feathers. Up jumped the fire, and out winked the candle.

Jumpy myself, I was back against the logs of the wall, my free hand on a shelf plank that was wedged there. The rain had whetted the clay chinking soft between the logs, and a muddy trickle fell on my fingers. I watched the fire, and its dirty gray smoke stirred and swelled, and a fat-looking puff crawled out of it like a live thing.

That smoke stayed in one bunch. It hung there, a sort of egg-shaped chunk of it, hanging above the stones of the hearth. I think the girl must have half fallen, then caught herself; for I heard the legs of the chair scrape on the puncheons. The smoke was molding itself, in what light I could make out, and began to look solid and shapy, as tall as me but thicker across, and two streamy coils waved out in the air like arms.

"Don't!" the girl was begging. "Don't let him—"

On that shelf at my hand stood a dish and an empty old bottle, the kind of bottle the old glassmakers blew a hundred years back. I grabbed up the dish. I saw that smoke shape drifting sort of slow and greedy, clear of the hearth, and betwixt those two wavy steamy arm coils rose up a lumpy head thing. There was enough firelight to see that this smoke was thicker than just smoke. It must have soot and ash dust in it, solid enough to choke you. And in the lumpy head hung two dull red sparks, like eyes.

Gentlemen, more than that you'd not care to have me tell you about it.

I flung the dish, and it sang through the room and it went straight for where I threw, but it didn't stop. It sailed right on past and into the fireplace, and I heard it smash to pieces on the stones. Where it had hit the smoke-shape, there showed a notchy hole all the way through, where the cheek would be on something alive. And whatever it was I'd thrown at, it never stopped its slow drift over to the table, gray and thick and horrible. And in the chimney the wind went up and down, like a dasher in a churn.

"No," the girl wailed again and moved back, dragging the chair with her.

Then all quick I saw what was in whatever that thing had for a mind. I ran at the table, too, and its spark-eyes flickered at us both. I felt a creeping hot smelly sense, like dirty ugly smoke. It made me feel sick and shaky-legged, but I made my eyes look back at those two glary sparks.

"Are you Forney Meechum?" I asked it. "Want to sit down at this dumb supper? Think it was laid out for you?"

It swayed back and forth, like a tree-branch, and outside the rain fell in its bucketfuls.

I moved around the table, holding out the guitar. I'd thought the smoky thing moved slow, but it was across the room to the other side the way a shadow flings itself when you move a lamp. I ran after it, quick as I could, and got to the door first.

"Not that way, either!"

I shooed it back with the guitar, and sketched a

cross on the glass pane. Then the wavy arm-streaks and the lumpy cloud of head and body went sliding back toward the table.

"Light that candle!" I hollered the girl. "Light it!"

She heard, and she grabbed up the candle from the table. She ran across the floor, the cloud hovering after her. Then she was down on her knee, putting the candle into the fireplace, and that quick it lighted up.

And there wasn't any smoke-shape anywhere in the room that now we could see plain.

"Where did he go?" she asked.

I looked round to see. He hadn't left by door or window, for I'd made my crosses there.

"He ran," I said. "He ran before us like a scared coward."

"But he was strong—" she started to say.

"He was bad," I put in, not very mannerly. "Badness thinks it's strong. But it's scared. Scared of lights, and crosses, and silver."

I picked at my guitar's silver strings, and making that music I walked round the room, and round again. For what was left of Forney Meechum must be hiding somewhere or other. And we'd best find out where he hid, or he'd be out at us again when we weren't ready.

I looked in the corners, up at the rafters. Then at the shelf. Then at the shelf again.

That old bottle a-standing there, it was dark-looking, like muddy water. Or like muddy water, and in the muddiness maybe a hiding thing, like what might hide in such a place; a snake or a worse thing than a snake, waiting its time.

I didn't want her to see too, so I made up something quick.

"Look over in the corner yonder," I said. "Take the candle."

She moved to look, and I moved to follow her. Close against a wall, I scraped from the clay clinking a wet gob as big as my thumb. I was within a long reach of the shelf.

"The corner," I said, pointing.

And, quick as I could make it, I shot out my arm and I jammed that clay down on top of the open bottle neck and shoved it in tight, like a cork.

"What—" she wondered.

I picked up the bottle. It felt warm and tingly. In the candle-light we could see the dark thick boiling cloud inside, a-stirring and a-spinning and a-fighting every whichaway, and no way out. I took the candle and dripped wax on the clay stopper, and in the wax I marked a cross with my thumb nail.

"Remember the Arabian Nights book?" I asked.

"No." She shook her coppery head. "What kind of book is it?"

"Has a thousand and one tales," I said. "And one tells how an evil spirit was tricked in a bottle like this, and sealed in there forever. We've got Forney Meechum safe."

She put the candle on the table. She pushed the chair back into place and stood behind it in her green dress, straight and tall and proud, the way I'd first seen her.

"Now he can come," she said to me, very sure. "Jeremiah."

"Jeremiah Donovant?" I asked, all wondered.

"Who else? He's coming back here to me, after all these years. I felt him coming."

"Then—" I said, but I never had to say it. By then, I knew who she was.

"I told you I wasn't all dead," reminded Lute Meechum. "Forney shot me in the heart and flung me in a lonely grave, but I couldn't all die. For love is stronger than death, John. And I just lay there till I knew for certain sure that Jeremiah was a-heading back here for me."

I took my coat from beside the fireplace. It felt

funny to be in that cabin, with one haunt inside the bottle and another standing behind the chair.

"Thank you for everything, John," she said, most mannerly. "Thank you kindly, and bless you. You can go now, it's all right."

The door squeaked open.

In out of the night came the wettest man you could ever think of. His shoulders and pant legs were soaked. Water dripped from his white hair and his old stubbly chin.

"Mr. Jay," I greeted him.

"Jeremiah," Lute Meechum greeted him.

He paid me no mind. He walked across. "I had to come, I reckon," he said to her, and the candle went out again.

But I could see him sinking down into the chair, and the light from the fireplace made his face look all of a sudden not old any more.

He put his face up, and she put hers down. Their faces came together. He went all slack and limp in the chair. He was at rest.

And I was outside with the bottle in one hand, my guitar in the other. There was nary cloud in the sky, and the moon shone down on me like a ball of white fire.

The cabin was dark inside now, and I saw by the moon that it was all wrecky. The roof fallen in, the window broken, the logs rotten and their chinking gone—you'd have sworn nobody had set a foot there for fifty years back. But inside, Jeremiah Donovant and Lute Meechum were together at last, and peaceful. So peaceful, I reckon most folks would call them dead and gone.

On along the trail I could see so clear now, I found a hollow tree. Down in its dark inside I put the bottle and left it there.

It seemed to me I ought to be shaky and scared, but I wasn't. I felt right good. That dumb supper now—the way I'd heard it told, sometimes a dumb supper calls up things that oughtn't be there; but now I'd seen a dead haunt, a-setting a dumb supper to tole a living man. And it wasn't a bad thing to do. It wasn't a wrong thing. They were happy about it, and happy about each other, I knew that for certain sure.

Walking in the bright moonlight, I began to strum my guitar. The song I sang is really an old, old one:

"Beauty, strength, youth, are flowers and fading seen—
 Duty, faith, love, are roots and ever green. . . ."

I CAN'T CLAIM THAT

When I called Joss Kift's witch-talk a lie, Joss swore he'd witch me to death in thirteen days.

Then in my path a rag doll looking like me, with a pin stuck in its heart. Then a black rooster flopping across my way with his throat cut, then a black dog hung to a tree, then other things. The thirteenth dawn, a whisper from nowhere that at midnight a stick with my soul in it would be broken thirteen times and burnt in a special kind of fire.

I lay on a pallet bed in Tram Colley's cabin, not moving, not speaking, not opening my mouth for the water Tram tried to spoon to me. Midnight. A fire blazed outside. Its smoke stunk. My friends around me heard the stick break and break and break, heard Joss laugh. Then Joss stuck his head in the window above me. "Ain't he natural-looking?" Joss snickered.

I grabbed his neck with both hands. Joss dropped and hung across the sill like a sock. When they touched him, his heart had stopped, scared out of its beating.

I got up. "Sorry he ended thataway," I said. "I made out that I was under his spell, to fool him."

Tram Colley looked at me alive and Joss dead. "He'll speak no more wild words and frightful commands," he said. "Witches can't prevail against a pure heart."

"I can't claim that," I said.

Because I can't. My heart's sinful. Each day I only hope it's less sinful than yesterday.

THE LITTLE BLACK TRAIN

Climbing from that soggy valley into the High Fork country, with peaks saw-toothing into the sky and hollows a-diving away down and trees thicketed every whichaway, you'd think human foot had never stepped. Walking the trail betwixt high pines, I touched my guitar's silver strings for company of the sound. But then a man squandered into sight around the bend ahead—young-like, red-faced, baldy-headed. Gentlemen, he was as drunk as a hoot. I gave him good evening.

"Can you play that there thing?" he gobbled at me, and, second grab of his shaky hand, he got hold of my hickory shirt sleeve. "Come to the party, friend. Our fiddle band, last moment, they got scared out. We got just only a mouth-harp left to play for us."

"What scared the fiddle band?" I asked him to tell.

"Party's at Miss Donie Carawan's," he said, without replying me. "Bobbycue hog and chicken, barrel of good blockader whiskey."

"Hark," I said, "ever hear tell of a man invited a stranger fiddler, he turned out to be Satan?"

"Shoo," he snickered, "Satan plays the fiddle. You play the guitar. I don't pay your guitar no worry. What's your name, friend?"

"John. What's yours?"

But he'd started up a narrow, grown-over, snaky-turny path you'd not notice. I reckoned the party'd be at a house, where I might could sleep the night that was coming, so I followed. He near about fell back on top of me, he was so stone drunk, but we got to a notch on the ridge, and the far side was a valley of trees, dark and secret looking. Going down, I heard loud laughing talk. Finally we came to a yard at the bottom. There was a house there, and it looked like enough men and women to swing a primary election.

So loud they whooped at us, it rang my ears. The drunk man waved both his hands. "This here's my friend John," he bawled, "and he's a-going to play us some music."

They whooped louder at that, so easiest thing for me to do was start picking *Hell Broke Loose in Georgia,* and right away they danced up a storm.

Wild they whipped and whirled. Most part of them were young folks dressed in their best. One side, a great big man called the dance, but you couldn't much hear him, everybody laughed and hollered so loud. It got in my mind that children laugh and yell thataway, a-passing an old burying ground with ghosts. It was the way they might could be trying to dance down the nervouses. I jumped myself, betwixt notes, when something started a-moaning beside me. But it was just a middling old fellow with a thin face, blowing his mouth-harp along with my guitar.

I looked to the house. It was new and wide and solid, with white-washed clay chinked betwixt the squared logs. Through a dog-trot from front to back I saw clear down valley, west to where the sunball dropped red toward a far string of mountains. The bottom's trees were spaced out with a kind of path or road, the whole length. The house windows began to light up as I played. Somebody was putting a match to lamps, against the fall of night.

End of the time, everybody clapped me loud and long. "More! More!" they hollered, bunched among the yard trees, still fighting their nervouses.

"Friends," I managed to be heard, "let me make my manners to the one who's giving this party."

"Hi, Miss Donie," yelled the drunk man. "Come meet John."

From the house she walked through the crowded-around folks, a-stepping so gay she looked taller than she was. A right much stripy skirt swished to her high heels, but she hadn't so much dress above, and none at all on her round arms and shoulders. The buttery yellow of her hair must have come from a bottle, and the doll pink of her face from a box. She smiled up to me, and her perfume tingled my nose. Behind her followed the big dance-caller, with his dead black hair and wide teeth, and his heavy hands a-swinging like balance weights.

"Glad you came, John," she said, deep in her round throat.

I looked on her robin-egg blue eyes and her red mouth and her bare pink shoulders. She was maybe forty, without looking so much. "Proud to be here," I said, my politest. "Is this a birthday, Miss Donie Carawan?"

Folks fell quiet, swapping looks. An open cooking fire blazed up as the night sneaked in. Donie Carawan laughed deep.

"Birthday of a curse," and she widened her blue eyes. "End of the curse, too, I reckon. All tonight."

Some mouths came open, but nary word came out. I reckoned that whatever scared out the fiddle band was right scary. She held out a slim hand with greeny-stoned rings on it.

"Come eat and drink, John," she bade me.

"Thanks," I said, for I'd not eaten ary mouthful since the night before.

Off she led me, her fingers a-pressing mine, her blue eyes a-watching me sideways. The big dance-caller glittered a glare after us. He acted jealoused up because she'd made me such a warm welcome.

Two dark-faced old men stood at an iron rack above the coal pit, where lay two halves of a slow-cooking hog. One old man dipped a stick with a rag ball into a sauce kettle and painted it over the brown roast meat. From a big pot of fat over another fire, an old woman forked out hush-puppies into pans set ready on a plank table.

"Line up!" called Donie Carawan out, like a bugle. They lined up, a-talking and a-hollering again, smiling their faces again. It was some way like dreams you have, folks a-carrying on and something bad a-coming on to happen.

Donie Carawan nestled her bare arm through my elbow while an old man sliced barbecued hog chunks on paper plates for us. The old woman forked on a hush-puppy and a big hobby of cole slaw. Eating, I wondered how they made that good barbecue sauce— wondered, too, if all these folks really wanted to be here for what Donie Carawan called the birthday curse.

"John," she said, the way you'd think she'd read what I wondered, "don't they say a witch's curse can't work against a pure heart?"

"They say that," I agreed her, and she laughed her laugh, and the big dance-caller and the skinny mouth-harp man looked up from their food.

"An old witch cursed me for guilty twenty years back," she said. "The law said I was innocent. Who was right?"

"Don't know how to answer that," I had to say, and again she laughed, and bit white teeth into her hush-puppy.

"Look round you, John," she said. "This is my house, and this is my valley, and these folks are my friends, come to help me pleasure myself."

Again I reckoned she was the only one there that was pleasured; or maybe not even her.

"Law me," she laughed, "it's rough on some few folks, a-holding their breath all these years to see that curse light on me. Since it didn't light, I figured how to shoo it away." Her blue eyes looked on me. "But what are you doing around High Fork, John?"

The dance-caller listened, and the thin mouth-harp man. "Just passing through," I said. "On my way to the highway over yonder, to catch a bus to Sky Notch, or somewhere near. But I look for songs, and I've heard tell of a High Fork song, something about a little black train."

Silence quick stretched all around, the way you'd think I'd been impolite. But yet again she laughed.

"I've known that song as long as I've known about the curse, near to," she said. "Want me to sing it for you?"

Folks watched us, and, "Please, ma'am," I said.

She sang, there in the yellow lamplight and red firelight, among the shadowy trees and the mountain dark, and no moon yet up overhead. Her voice was a good voice. I put down my plate and, a line or two along, I made out to follow her with the guitar:

> "I heard a voice of warning,
> A message from on high,
> 'Go put your house in order,
> For thou shalt surely die.
> Tell all your friends a long farewell
> And get your business right—
> The little black train is rolling in
> To call for you tonight....' "

"That's a tuneful thing," I said. "Sounds like a train a-rolling."

"My voice isn't high enough to sound the whistle part," she smiled at me, red-mouthed.

"I might could do that," softly said the mouth-harp man, coming close. Folks craned at us, looking sick, embarrassed, purely distasteful. I wondered why I shouldn't have spoken of that black train song.

But then rose a holler near the house, where a barrel was set. The drunk man that had fetched me was yelling mad at another man near about as drunk, and they were a-trying to grab a drinking gourd from one another. Two-three other men on each side hoorawed them on.

"Jeth," said Donie Carawan to the big dance-caller. "Let's stop that before they spill the whiskey, Jeth."

Jeth and she headed for the bunch by the barrel, and everybody else crowded to watch.

"John," said the quiet mouth-harp man, with firelight showing lines in his thin face, salty gray in his hair. "What you really doing here?"

"I'm a-watching," I said, while big Jeth hauled the two drunk men apart from each other, and Donie Carawan scolded them. "And a-listening," I said. "A-wanting to know how the black train song fits in with this party and that tale about the curse. You know how?"

"I know."

We carried our food out of the firelight. Folks were a-crowding to the barrel, to drink and laugh and yell.

"Donie Carawan was to marry Trevis Jones," the mouth-harp man told me. "He owned the High Fork Railroad that freighted the timber from this valley. But," and he swallowed hard, "another young fellow loved her—Cobb Richardson, who ran Trevis Jones' train on the High Fork Railroad. And he killed Trevis Jones."

"For love?" I inquired him.

"Folks reckoned that Donie Carawan love-talked Cobb into the killing; for Trevis had made a will and heired her all his money and property—the railroad and all. But Cobb made confession, said Donie had no part in it. The law let her go, and killed Cobb in the electric chair, down at the state capital."

"I declared to never," I said.

"Fact. And Cobb's mother, Mrs. Amanda Richardson, spoke the curse."

"Oh," I said, "was she the witch who—"

"She was no witch," he broke me off, "but she cursed Donie Carawan, that the train that Cobb drove, and Trevis had heired to her, would be her death and destruction. Donie just laughed—you've heard her laugh. And folks started that black train song."

"Who made it?" I asked him.

"Reckon I did," he said, and looked long at me. "Maybe it was the song decided Donie Carawan to deal with the Hickory River Railroad, agree them for an income of money not to run the High Fork train no more."

I'd finished my barbecue. I didn't feel like asking for more of it. "I see," I told him. "She reckoned that if no train ran on the High Fork tracks, it couldn't be her death and destruction."

We put our plates on one of the fires. It seemed to me that the other folks quieted down their laughing and talking as the night got darker.

"But folks say the train runs on its track," the mouth-harp man went on. "A black train, some nights at midnight, they say. And when it runs, a sinner dies."

"You ever see it run?"

"No, John, but I've sure God heard it. And only Donie Carawan laughs about it."

She laughed right then, joking the two drunk men who'd feathered up to fight. Ary man's neck craned at her, and the women didn't look to be relishing that. My neck craned some, itself.

"Twenty years back, the height of her bloom," said the mouth-harp man, "and you'd never look at any woman else but her."

"What does she mean, no more curse?"

"Well, she sold off the rails of the High Fork Road, that's stood idle for twenty years. This day the last of them was tore up and fetched off. Meanwhile, she's had this house built, right across where the right of way used to be. Looky yonder, through the dog-trot. That's where the road ran."

So it was the old road bed that made the dark dip amongst the trees. Just now it didn't look so wide a dip.

"No more rails," he said. "She reckons, no black train at midnight. Folks came at her bidding, some because they rent land from her, some because they owe her money, and some—men folks—because they'll do ary thing she calls for."

"And she never married?" I asked.

"If she done that, she'd lose the money and land she heired from Trevis Jones. It was in his will. So she just takes men without a-marrying, one and then another. I've known men kill theirselves just because she put her heart back in her pocket on them. Lately here, it's been big Jeth. Tonight she acts like picking herself a new one."

She walked back through the lamplight and firelight. "These folks want to dance again, John," she said.

I played *Many Thousands Gone*, with the mouth-harp to help, and they stomped like a many thousands dancing. In its thick, Donie Carawan promenaded left and right and do-si-doed with a fair-haired young fellow, and Jeth the dance-caller looked sour as pickles. When I'd done, Donie Carawan swished back to me.

"Let just the mouth-harp play and dance with me, John."

"I'm no powerful dancer," I said. "Just now, I'd relish to practice the black train song."

Her blue eyes crinkled. "All right. Play, and I'll sing."

She did. The mouth-harp man blew moany whistles to my guitar, and folks listened, a-goggling like frogs:

> "A bold young man kept mocking,
> Cared not for the warning word,
> When the wild and lonesome whistle
> Of the little black train he heard.

> 'Have mercy, Lord forgive me,
>   I'm cut down in my sin!
> O death, will you not spare me?—'
> But the little black train rolled in...."

And she laughed like before, deep and bantering. Jeth the dance-caller made a funny sound in his bull throat.

"What I don't figure, John," he said, "is how you made the train sound like a-coming closer and closer."

"Just changed the music," I told him. "Changed the pitch."

"Fact," said the mouth-harp man. "I played the change with him."

A woman laughed, nervous. "Now I think, that's the truth. A train whistle sounds higher and higher when it comes up to you. Then it passes and goes off away, sounding lower and lower."

"I never heard the train go away in the song," allowed a man beside her. "It just kept coming." And he shrugged, maybe he shivered.

"Miss Donie," said the woman, "reckon I'll go along."

"Stay on, Lettie," Donie Carawan told her instead of asking.

"Got a right much walking to do, and no moon up," said the woman. "Reuben, you come on with me."

She left. The man looked back just once at Donie Carawan, then he left too. Another couple, then another, went with them from the firelight. Maybe more would have gone, but Donie Carawan snorted, like a horse, to make them stay.

"Let's drink," she said. "Plenty for all, now those folks I reckoned to be my friends have gone."

Two-three others faded away, between there and the barrel. Donie Carawan dipped herself a drink, watching me over the gourd's edge. Then she dipped more and held it out.

"When you drink after a lady you're getting a kiss," she whispered.

I drank. It was good blockader liquor. "Tasty," I said.

"The kiss?" she laughed. But the dance-caller didn't laugh, nor either the mouth-harp man, nor yet me.

"Let's dance," she said, and I picked *Sourwood Mountain* and the mouth-harp moaned with me. The dancers had got to be few, just in a short while. But the trees they danced through looked bigger, and more of them. It minded me of how I'd heard, when I was a chap, about day trees and night trees, they weren't the same at all; and the night trees can crowd all round a house they don't like, pound the shingles off the roof, bust in the window glass and the door panels; and on such a night you'd better never set your foot outside. . . .

Not so much clapping at the end, not such hollerings of "More!" Folks went for another drink at the barrel, but the mouth-harp man held me back.

"Tell me that business," he said. "The noise sounding higher when the train's a-rolling close."

"It was explained me by a man I know, place in Tennessee called Oak Ridge. It's with what they call sound waves, and some way it works with light, too. Don't rightly catch on how, but they measure how far it is to the stars thataway."

He frowned. "Something like what they call radar?"

"No," I shook my head. "No machinery to it. It's what they call a principle. Fellow named Doppler—Christian Doppler, a foreigner—got it up."

"His name was Christian," the mouth-harp man said. "Then I don't reckon it's witch business."

"Why you worrying it?"

"I was a-watching through the dog-trot when we played that black train song, changing the pitch, making it sound like a-coming near. Looky yonder, John, see for yourself."

I looked. There was a streaky shine down the valley, a-picking up the light of the moon that was just before to come up. I saw what he meant. It was as if those pulled-up rails were still there, where they'd been gone before.

"That second verse Miss Donie sang," I said. "Was it about—"

"Yes," he said before I'd finished. "That was about Cobb Richardson. How he prayed for God's forgiveness, the night before he died."

Donie Caraway came and poked her hand under my arm. That good strong liquor was feeling its way round inside her. She laughed at almost nothing whatever. "You're not a-leaving, anyway," she smiled at me.

"Don't have any place to go in a hurry," I said.

She upped on her pointed toes. "Stay here tonight," she said in my ear. "The rest will be gone by midnight."

"You invite men like that?" I said, looking into her blue eyes. "When you don't know them?"

"I know men," she said. "Knowing men keeps me young." Her fingers touched my guitar, and the strings whispered. "Sing me something."

"I still want to learn that black train song."

"But I've sung you both verses."

"Then," I said, "I'll sing a verse I've just now made up." I looked at the mouth-harp man. "Help me with this."

Together we played, raising pitch gradually, and I sang the new verse I made, with my eyes on Donie Carawan.

"Go tell that laughing lady
All filled with wordly pride,
The little black train is coming,
Get ready to take a ride.
With a little black coach and engine

> And a little black baggage car,
> The words and deeds she has said and done
> Must roll to the judgment bar. . . ."

And I looked up at those who'd stayed. They weren't more than a few now, bunched up like cows in a storm; all except Big Jeth, a-standing one side with eyes stabbing me, and Donie Carawan, a-leaning tired like to a tree.

"Jeth," she said, "stomp that guitar to pieces."

I switched the carrying cord off my neck and held the guitar at my side. "Don't try it, Jeth," I warned him.

His big square teeth grinned, with dark spaces betwixt them. He looked twice as broad as me. "I'll stomp you and it both."

I put the guitar on the ground, glad I'd had but the one drink. Jeth ran and stooped for it, and I put my fist hard under his ear. He hopped two steps away to keep on his feet.

Shouldn't any man name me what he did then, and I hit him twice more. His nose flatted out under my knuckles. When he pulled back away, blood trickled.

The mouth-harp man had grabbed up my guitar. "This here'll be a square fight," he said, louder than he'd spoken so far. "Ain't a fair one, Jeth's so big, but it'll be square—just them two in it, and no more!"

"I'll settle you later," Jeth promised him.

"Settle me first," I said, and got betwixt them.

Jeth ran at me. I stepped sidewise and got him under the ear as he went shammocking past. He turned, and I dug my fist right into his belly-middle to stir up that liquor he'd drunk, then the other fist under the ear yet once more, then on the chin and the mouth and the broken nose—ten licks like that, as fast and hard as I could fetch them. Eighth or ninth he went slack, and the tenth he just fell flat and loose, like a coat off a nail. I stood waiting, but he didn't move on the ground.

"Gentlemen," said the drunk man who'd fetched me, "looky yonder at Jeth laying there. Never figured to see the day. Maybe that stranger a-naming himself John is Satan after all!"

Donie Carawan walked across the gouged Jeth's ribs with the pointy toe of her high-heeled shoe. "Get up," she bade him.

He grunted and mumbled and opened his eyes. Then he got up, joint by careful joint, like a sick bull. He tried to stop the blood from his nose with the back of his big hand. Donie Carawan looked at him and then she looked at me.

"Get off my place, Jeth," she ordered.

He went, cripply-like, with his knees bent and his hands loose and his back humped, the way you'd think he carried a heavy burden.

"Reckon I'll go too," hiccuped the drunk man.

"Then go!" Donie Carawan yelled at him. "All of you go, right now, this minute! I see I don't have a friend in the whole lot! Hurry up, get going, everybody!"

Hands on hips, she blared it out. The others moved off through the trees, faster than Jeth had gone. But I stood where I was. The mouth-harp man gave me back my guitar, and I touched a chord on its strings. Donie Carawan spun round like a top to set her blue eyes on me.

"You stayed," she said, as if she thought it was funny.

"It's not midnight yet," I told her.

"But near to," added the mouth-harp man. "Just a few minutes off. And at midnight the little black train comes a-running."

She lifted her round bare shoulders. She made to laugh, but didn't.

"That's gone. If it ever was true, it's not true any more. The rails were taken up—"

"Looky through the dog-trot," the mouth-harp

man broke in. "Them two rails is a-streaking along the valley."

She swung back and she looked, and it seemed to me she swayed in the light of the dying fires. She saw those streaky rails.

"And hark," said the mouth-harp man. "Don't youins hear it?"

I heard it. So did Donie Carawan, for she flinched. It was a wild and lonesome whistle, soft but plain, far down valley.

"Are you doing that, John?" she squeaked at me, her voice gone all of a sudden high and weak and old. Then she ran at the house and into the dog-trot, staring down along what looked like railroad track.

I followed her and the mouth-harp man followed me. Inside the dog-trot the dirt floor was trod down, hard as brick. Donie Carawan looked at us. Lamplight through a window made her face look pale, with the painted red of her mouth almost black against it.

"You're playing a trick, John," she said.

"Not me," I swore to her.

It whistled—*wooooooeeee!* And I looked along the two rails, a-shining plain as plain in the light of the rising moon, to curve off round the valley-bend. Next second, the engine sounded, *chuckchuckchuckchuck*, and again the whistle, *woooooooooeeeee!*

"Miss Donie," I said, close behind her, "you'd better go away."

I pushed her gently.

"No!" she lifted her fists. I saw cordy lines on their backs, they weren't young fists. "It's my house—my land—and it's my railroad!"

"But you sold the rails—"

"If it comes here, where can I run to from it?"

"I'm going, John," said the mouth-harp man. "You and me raised the pitch and fetched the black train. Thought I could stay, watch and glory on it. But I ain't man enough."

Going, he blew a moany whistle on his mouth-harp,

and the other whistle blew back a reply, *woooooooeeee!*
Higher in the pitch.

"That's a real train," I told Donie Carawan.

"No," she said, her voice dead-sounding. "It's heading here, but it's no real train. Look, John—on the ground."

Something like rails ran there, right through the dog-trot like through a tunnel. Maybe it was some peculiar way of the moonlight. They lay close together, like narrow-gauge rails. I didn't feel like touching my toe to them to make sure of them. Holding my guitar under my arm, I took Donie Carawan's smooth bare elbow in my other hand. "We'd better go," I said again.

"I can't."

She said it loud and sharp and scared. And her arm was like the rail of fence, it was so stiff and unmoving.

"I won't leave," she was saying. "I own this land."

I tried to pick her up, and that couldn't be done. You'd have thought she'd grown to the ground in that dog-trot, spang betwixt what looked like the rails, you'd figure roots had come from her pointy toes and high heels. Out yonder, where the tracks curved off, the sound rose louder, higher, *chuckchuckchuck chuck—wooooooeeee!* And the light was a-shining round the curve, like a headlight only with blue to its yellow.

The engine-sound made the notes of the song in my head:

"Go put your house in order,
For thou shalt surely die. . . ."

Getting higher, higher, changing pitch as it came close and closer—

I don't know when I began picking the tune on my guitar, but I played as I stood there with Donie Carawan. She couldn't flee. She was rooted there, or frozen there, and the train was a-going to come in sight any second.

The mouth-harp man had credited us with fetching it, with that change of pitch. And, whatever anybody might could deserve, it wasn't for me to bring their deservings on them. I thought that, and:

Christian Doppler, who'd thought out the wherefore of how pitch brings the sound of closeness, had a name that couldn't go with witchery. Then if an honest man tried—

I slid my fingers up the guitar-neck, little by little, as I picked the music. And the pitch sneaked down.

"Here it comes, John," whimpered Donie Carawan, standing like a stump.

"No," I said. "It's going. Listen."

I played so soft you could pick up the train noise with your ear. And the pitch dropped, like with my guitar, and the whistle sounded—*woooooeee!*—lower it sounded.

"The light," she said. "Dimmer—oh, if I had the chance to live different—"

She moaned and swayed. Words came for me to sing as I picked:

> "Oh, see her standing helpless,
> Oh, hear her crying tears.
> She's counting her last moments
> As once she counted years.
> She'll turn from proud and wicked ways,
> She'll turn from sin, O Lord,
> If the little black train will just back up
> And not take her aboard. . . ."

She wept, all right. I heard her breath catch and strangle and shake her, near about tearing her ribs loose from her backbone. I picked on, strummed on, lower and lower.

Just for a wink, I thought I could glimpse what might could have come rolling at us.

THE LITTLE BLACK TRAIN 179

It was little, all right, and under that funny cold-blue light it was black. And the cars weren't bigger than coffins, and some way they looked like coffins. Or either I just sort of imagined that, dreamed it while I stood there. Anyway, the light grew dim, and the *chuckchuckchuckchuck* went softer and lower, and you'd guess the train was a-backing off, out of hearing.

I stopped my hand on the silver strings. We stood there in a silence like what must be on the lifeless, airless moon.

Then Donie Carawan gave out one big, broken sob, and I caught her with my free arm as she fell.

She was soft enough then. All the tight was gone out of her. She lifted one weak, round bare arm around my neck, and her tears wet my hickory shirt.

"You saved me, John, you turned the curse away."

"I reckon so," I said, though that sounded like a brag. I looked down at the rails, and they weren't there, in the dog-trot or either beyond. Just the floor of the valley, and moonlight in it now. The cooking fires had burnt out, and in the house the lamps were low.

Her arm tightened around me. "Come in," she said. "Come in, John. We're alone now."

"I'm going to head off away," I said.

Her arm dropped from me. "What's the matter? Don't you like me?"

"Miss Donie," I said, "I turned that curse from you. It didn't die. You can't kill it by a-laughing at it, or a-saying there aren't such things, or by pulling up rails. It held off tonight. But it might could come back."

"What must I do?" she said, and half-raised her arms to me again.

"Stop your bad way of life."

Her blue eyes got round in her pale face.

"You do want me to live," she said, hopeful.

"Yes. You said that folks owe you money, rent land

from you. How would they make out if you got carried off?"

She saw what I meant, maybe for the first time in her life.

"Try to help the folks," I said. "There's a thousand ways.

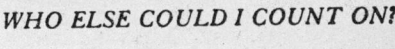
WHO ELSE COULD I COUNT ON?

reckon I believe you," I admitted to the old man at last. "You've given me proofs. It couldn't be any otherwise but that you've come back from times forty years ahead of now."

"You can believe wonders, John," he said. "Not many could be made to believe the things I've told."

"This war that's coming," I started to say, "the one that nobody will win—"

"The war that everybody will lose," he said. "I've come back to this day and time to keep it from starting, if I can. Come with me, John, we'll go to the rulers of this world. We'll make them believe, too, make them see that the war mustn't start."

"Explain me one thing first," I said, and: "What's that?" he asked.

"If you were an old man forty years along from now, then you'd have been young right in these times." I talked slowly, trying to clear the thought for both of us. "If that's so, what if you meet the young man you used to be?"

So softly he smiled: "John," he said, "why do you reckon I sought you out of all living men today?"

"Lord have mercy!" I said.

"Who else could I count on?"

"Lord have mercy!" I said again.

WALK LIKE A MOUNTAIN

Once at Sky Notch, I never grudged the trouble getting there. It was so purely pretty, I was glad outlanders weren't apt to crowd in and spoil all.

The Notch cut through a tall peak that stood against a higher cliff. Steep brush faces each side, and a falls at the back that made a trickly branch, and five pole cabins along the waterside. Corn patches, a few pigs in pens, chickens running round, a cow tied up one place. It wondered me how they ever got the cow up there. Laurels grew, and climby vines, and mountain flowers in bunches and sprawls. Nobody moved in the yards or at the doors, though, so I stopped by a tree and hollered the first house.

"Hello, the house!" I called. "Hello to the man of the house and all inside."

A plank door opened about an inch. "Hello to yourself," a pretty voice replied me. "Who's out yonder with the guitar?"

I moved from under the tree. "My name's John. Does Mr. Lane Jarrett live hereabouts? Got word for him, from his old home place on Drowning Creek."

The door opened wider, and there stood a skimpy little man with gray whiskers. "That's funny," he said.

The funnyness I didn't see. I'd known Mr. Lane Jarrett years back, before he and his daughter Page moved to Sky Notch. When his uncle Jeb died and heired him some money, I'd agreed to bear it to Sky

Notch, and gentlemen, it was a long, weary way getting there.

First a bus, up and down and through mountains, stop at every pig trough for passengers. I got off at Charlie's Jump, and who Charlie was or why or when he jumped, nobody there can tell you. Climbed a high ridge, got down the far side then a twenty-devil way along a deep valley river. Up another height, another beyond that. Then it was night and nobody would want to climb more, because it was grown up with the kind of trees that the dark melts in around you. I made a fire and ate my supper rations I'd brought. Woke at dawn and climbed up and down and up, and here I was.

"Funny, about Lane Jarrett," gritted the little man out. "You come about that there business?"

I looked up the walls of the Notch. Their tops were toothy rocks, and the walls like two jaws, near about to bite on what was caught betwixt them. Right then the Notch didn't look so pretty.

"Can't rightly say, sir," I told him, "till I know what business you mean."

"Rafe Enoch!" He boomed the name out, like firing two barrels of a gun. "That's what I mean!" He came out, puny in his jeans and no shoes on his feet. "I'm Oakman Dillon. Your name's John? Why you got that guitar?"

"I pick it some," I replied him. "And I sing." Tweaking the silver strings, I sang a few lines:

> "By the shores of Lonesome River
> Where the waters ebb and flow,
> Where the wild red rose is budding
> And the pleasant breezes blow,
> It was there I spied the lady
> That forever I adore,
> And she was lonesome walking
> On the Lonesome River shore..."

"Rafe Enoch," he grated out again. "Fetched off Miss Page Jarrett like she was a banty chicken!"

Slap, I quieted the strings with my palm. "Mr. Lane's little daughter Page was stolen away?"

He sat down on the door log. "She ain't suchy little daughter, John. She's six foot maybe three inches —tall as you, taller even. Best-looking big woman you ever see. Brown hair like home-cured tobacco, eyes green and bright as a fresh-squoze grape pulp."

"Fact?" I said, thinking Page must have changed a right much from the long-leggy little girl I'd known, must have grown tall like her daddy and dead mother, only taller. "Is this Rafe Enoch so big, a girl like that is right for him?"

"She's puny for him. He's near about eight foot tall, I judge." Oakman Dillon's gray whiskers stuck out like a mad cat's. "He grabbed her last evening where she walked by the fall, and up them rocks he clomb like a possum up a jackoak."

"Mr. Lane's a friend of mine," I said. "Can I help?"

"Nobody can't help, John. Rafe Enoch lives up at the top yonder." He jerked his head at the falls. "Been there a long spell—years, I reckon, since he run off from some place. Heard tell he broke a circus man's neck for offering him a job with a show. He built up there, top the falls, and he used to get along with us. Thanked us kindly for a mess of beans or roasting ears. But of late he's been mean-talking."

"Nobody mean-talked him back? I count five homes in this Notch. That means five grown men—can't they handle one giant?"

"Giant size ain't all Rafe Enoch's got." Again the whiskers bristled up. "Why he's got power and can make rain fall—"

"No," I put in quick. "Can't even science men do that for sure."

"I ain't studying science men. Rafe Enoch says for rain to fall and down it comes, the hour of day or night he speaks. Could drown us out of this here Notch if he took the mind."

"And he's fetched off Page Jarrett," I came back to what he'd said.

"That's the whole truth, John. Up he went with her in the evening, daring us to follow."

"Where are the other Notch folks?" I asked.

"Up yonder by the falls. Since dawn we've been a-wrestling Lane Jarrett back from climbing up and getting his neck twisted by Rafe. I came home to feed my hogs, now I'm heading back."

"I'll go with you," I said.

The falls dropped down a height as straight up as a chimney, and a many times taller, and their waters boiled off down the branch. Either side, the big boulder rocks piled on each other like stones in a big wall. Looking up, I saw a boil of clouds in the sky, dark and heavy, and I remembered what Oakman Dillon had said about big Rafe Enoch's rainmaking.

A bunch of folks stood there, and one was Mr. Lane Jarrett, bald on top and bigger than the rest. I touched his arm and he turned.

"John! Ain't seen you a way-back time. Let me make you known to these here folks."

He named their first names—Yoot, Ollie, Bill, Duff, Miss Lulie, Miss Sara May and so on. I said I had a pocketful of money for him, but he just nodded and asked did I know what was going on.

"Looky up against them clouds, John. See that pointy rock? My girl Page is on it."

The rock stuck out like a rooster's spur. Somebody was scrouched down on it, with the clouds blackening above and a long drop below.

"I see her blue dress," allowed Oakman Dillon, squinting. "How long she been up there, Lane?"

"I spotted her at sunup," said Mr. Lane. "She must have got away from Rafe Enoch in the night and crope out there. I'm going up."

He started to shinny up a rock, and Lord, the laugh that came down on us! It was clear and strong as a big splash of water, and like cold water it made us to shiver. Oakman Dillon caught Mr. Lane's ankle and yanked him down.

"Ain't a God's thing you can do, with him waiting up there," Oakman Dillon argued, and I grabbed Mr. Lane's elbow.

"Let me go," I said.

"You're a stranger, John, you ain't got no pick in this."

"But that big Rafe Enoch would know if it was you or Mr. Dillon or one of these others a-climbing. I'm strange to him, and he might be wondered about me and let me get all the way up. And once up, I might could do something."

"Leave him try it," said Oakman Dillon to that.

"Yes," said one of the lady-folks.

I slung my guitar behind me and took to the rocks. No peep of noise from anywhere, for maybe a minute's climbing. I got on about the fifth or sixth rock from the bottom, and that clear laugh ripped the sky far over my head.

"Name yourself!" roared down the voice that had laughed.

I looked up. How high was the top I couldn't say, but I made out a head and shoulders looking down, and knew they were another sight bigger head and shoulders than ever I'd seen on mortal man.

"Name yourself!" he yelled again, and in the black clouds a lightning flash wiggled, like a snake caught fire.

"John!" I yelled back.

"What you aim to do, John?"

Another lightning crack, that for a second seemed to peel off the clouds right and left. Nowhere to get away should lightning strike at me. On notion, I pulled my guitar to me and picked and sang:

"Went to the rock to hide my face,
The rock cried out, 'No hiding place.' . . ."

Gentlemen, the laugh was like the thunder after the lightning.

"Climb up, John," he hollered me. "I'll wait on you up here!"

I swarmed and swarved and scrabbled my way up, never looking down. Over my head that rock-sput got bigger. I figured it for maybe twelve-fifteen feet long, and on it I made out Page Jarrett in her blue dress. Oakman Dillon was right, she was purely big and purely good-looking. She sat on the pointy end of the rock and clung to it with her two long hands.

"Page," I said to her, with what breath I had left, and she looked with her green eyes and gave me an inch of smile. She looked to have a right much of her daddy's natural sand in her craw.

"John," boomed the thunder-voice, close above me now. "I asked you a while back, why you coming up?"

"To see how you make the rain fall," I said, under the ledge's overhand. "Give me a help up."

Down came a bare brown honey-hairy arm, and a hand the size of a scoop shovel. It got my wrist and snatched me like a turnip out of a patch, and I landed on my feet on broad flat stones.

Below yawned up those rock-toothed tops of the Notch's jaws. Inside them the brush and trees looked mossy and puny. The cabins were like baskets, the pigs and the cow like play-toys, and the branch so narrow you might could bridge it with your shoe. Shadow fell on the Notch from the fattening dark clouds.

Rafe Enoch stood over me like a sycamore over a wood shed. He was the almightiest big thing I'd ever seen on two legs.

Eight foot high, Oakman Dillon had said true enough, and thick-made in keeping. Shoulders to fill a barn door, and legs like tree trunks with fringy buckskin pants on them, and on his big feet mocassins of bear's hide with the fur on. His shirt, sewed together of pelts—fox, coon, the like of that—hadn't any sleeves, and hung open from his chest that was as broad as a cotton bale. Topping all, his face put you in mind of the full moon with a big yellow beard, but healthy-tanned, not pale like the moon. Big and dark eyes, and through the yellow beard his teeth grinned like big white sugar lumps.

"Maybe I ought to charge you to look at me," he said.

I recollected he'd struck a man dead for wanting him in a show, and I looked elsewhere. First at Page Jarrett on the rock spur. The wind from the clouds waved her brown hair like a flag, and fluttered her blue skirt around her drawn-up feet. Then I looked at the broad space above the falls.

From there I saw there was a right much of higher country, and just where I stood with Rafe Enoch was a big shelf, like a lap, with slopes behind it. In the middle of the flat space stood Rafe Enoch's house, built wigwam style of big old logs leaned together and chinked betwixt with clay and twigs. No trees to amount to aught on the shelf—just one behind the wigwam-house, and to its branches hung joints that looked like smoke meat.

"You hadn't picked your guitar so clever, maybe I'd not have saved you," said Rafe Enoch's thunder voice.

"Saved me?" I repeated him.

"Look." His big club finger pointed to the falls, then to the down-hugging clouds. "When they get together, what happens?"

Just at the ledge lip, where the falls went over, stones looked halfway washed out. A big shove of water would take them out the other half way, and the whole thing would pour down on Sky Notch.

"Why do this to the folks?" I asked.

He shook his yellow-curled head. "John, this is one rain I never called for. Sure enough, I can make rain, but sometimes it comes without me." He put one pumpkin-sized fist into his other palm. "That kind of rain I can't start or either stop, I just know it's coming. I've known about this one for days. It'll drown out Sky Notch like a rat nest."

I thought of Forney Meechum, who'd also made rain come, and who'd died a death as ugly as his doings. "Why didn't you tell them?" I asked.

"I tried to tell her." His eyes cut around to where Page Jarrett hung to the pointy rock, and his fingers raked his yellow beard. "She was a-walking by herself alone. I know how it feels to be alone. But when I told her, she called me a liar. I fetched her up here to save her, and she fought me." A grin. "She fought me better than I was ever fought by human soul. But she can't fight me hard enough."

"Can't you do aught about the storm?" I asked him.

"Can do this." He snapped his big fingers, and lightning crawled through the clouds just over us. I turtled my neck inside my shirt collar. Rafe Enoch twitched nary eyebrow.

"Rafe, you might could persuade the folks," I said. "They're not your size, but they're human like you."

"Then?" He roared his laugh. "They ain't like me, nor you ain't like me, though you're longer-made than common. Page yonder, she looks to have some of the Genesis giant blood in her. That's why I saved her life."

"Genesis giant blood," I repeated him, remembering the sixth chapter of Genesis. " 'There were giants in the earth in those days.' "

"That's it," said Rafe. "When the sons of God took wives of the daughters of men—their children were the mighty men of old, the men of renown. That's not the exact quote, but it's close enough."

He sat on a rock, near about as tall sitting as I was

standing. "Ary giant knows he was born from the sons of the gods," he said. "My name tells it, John."

I figure it. "Rafe—Raphah, the giant whose son was Goliath. And Enoch—"

"Or Anak. Remember the sons of Anak, and them scared-out spies sent into Canaan? They was grasshoppers in the sight of the sons of Anak, and more ways than just size." He sniffed. "They got scared back into the wilderness for forty long years. And Goliath!"

"David killed him," I dared remind.

"By a trick. A slingshot stone. Else David wouldn't have lasted longer than that."

His fingers snapped, and lightning winged over us like a hawk over a chicken run, I tried not to scrouch down.

"Why fight little old human men," he said, "when the blood of the sons of the gods is in you?"

I allowed he minded me of Strap Buckner with that talk.

"Who's Strap Buckner? What way do I mind you of him?"

I picked up the guitar, I sang the song:

"Strap Buckner he was called, he was more than
    eight feet tall.
And he walked like a mountain among men.
He was good and he was great, and the glorious
    Lone Star State
Will never look upon his like again. . . ."

"Strap Buckner had the strength of ten lions," I said, "and he used it as ten lions. Scorned to fight ordinary folks, so he challenged old Satan himself, skin for skin, on the banks of the Brazos. If Satan hadn't fought foul—"

"Another dirty fighter?" Rafe got up from where he sat, quick as quick for all his size. "Foul or not, Satan could never whip me!"

"Might be he couldn't," I judged, looking at Rafe. "But anyway, the Notch folks never hurt you. Used to give you stuff to eat."

"Don't need their stuff to eat," he said, the way you'd think that was the only argument. He waved past his wigwam-house. "Down yonder in some hollows, where ain't no human ever been, excepting maybe once the Indians. I hoe some corn there, some potatoes. I pick wild salad greens here and yonder. I kill me a deer, a bear, a wild hog. Ain't no human man ever got nerve to face them big wild hogs, but I chunk them with a rock or fling a sharp ash sapling, and what I fling at I fetch down. In the pond here I spear fish. Don't need their stuff to eat."

"Need it or not, why let them drown out?"

His face darkened, the way a moon darkens in a cloud. "Can't abide little folks' little eyes looking on me, wondering theirselves about me, thinking I'm not rightly natural."

He waited for me to say something, and it took nerve to say it.

"You're not a natural man, Rafe. You yourself allow you come from different blood. Paul Bunyan thought that same thing."

He grinned his big teeth. Then: "Page Jarrett," he called out, "better come off that their rock before the rain makes it slippy and you fall off. I'll help you—"

"Stay where you are, Rafe Enoch," she called back. "John can help me."

I went to the edge of that long drop down. The wind blew from above or below or maybe behind or before. I reached out my guitar, and Page crawled to where she could lay hold, and I helped her to the solid standing. She stood beside me, an inch or so taller, and she put a burning mean eye on Rafe Enoch. He made out he didn't notice.

"Paul Bunyan," he recollected what I'd said. "I've heard tell of him, the champion logger in the northern states."

"Bigger than you. I reckon," I said.

"Not bigger!" thundered Rafe.

"Anyway as big. But Rafe, why do you say you despise to be looked on by folks?"

"Just by little folks, John. Page Jarrett can look on me if she has the wish."

She looked off him, and drew herself up proud. Right then she appeared to be taller than what Oakman Dillon reckoned her, and I'm honest to say, gentlemen, she was a beauty-looking thing. Over us hung the clouds, loose and close, like a tent. I could feel the closeness around me, like water when you've waded up to your mouth-line.

"How soon does the rain start falling?" I asked Rafe.

"Right soon," said Rafe, pulling a grass stalk to bite in his big teeth. "Now Page is safe off that rocky point, it don't differ me a shuck when it falls."

"But when?" I asked again. "You know."

"Sure enough I know." He walked toward the pond, and me with him. I felt Page Jarrett's grape-green eyes a-digging our backs. The pond water was tarry black from reflecting the clouds. "Sure enough," said Rafe. "I know that, I know a right much. You natural humans, you know so pitiful little I'm sorrowed for you."

"Why not teach us?" I asked, and he snorted like a mean horse.

"Giants are reckoned stupid. Remember the tales? Your name's John, do you call to mind a tale about a man named, Jack, long back in time?"

"Jack the Giant Killer," I nodded. "Trapped a giant in a hole—"

"Cormoran," said Rafe. "Jack dug a pit in front of Cormoran's door. And Blunderbore he tricked into stabbing himself with a knife. But how did he do them things? He blew a horn to tole Cormoran out, and he ate at Blunderbore's table like a friend before tricking him to death." A louder snort. "More foul fighting. Did you climb up here to be Jack the Giant

Killer? Got some foul tricks? If that's it, you've done drove your ducks to the wrong puddle."

"More than a puddle here." I looked at the clouds and then across the pond. "Yonder, where the water edge comes above that little slanty slope—if it was open there, enough would run off to keep the Notch from flooding."

"Could be done," he nodded his big curly head, "if you had machinery to hoist the rocks out. But they're bigger than them fall rocks, they ain't half washed out to begin with. And there ain't no machinery, so just forget it, John. The Notch gets drowned out, with most of the folks living in it—all of them, if the devil bids high enough. Sing us a song while we wait for it to come to pass."

I whispered the strings with my thumb. "Thinking about John Henry," I said. "He wouldn't need a machine to open a drain yonder."

"How did he work?" asked Rafe.

"Had him a hammer twice the size other men swung," I said. "He drove steel when they cut the Big Bend Tunnel through Cruze Mountain. Outdrove the steam drill they fetched to compete him out of his job."

"Steam drill," Rafe growled. "They'd do that, them little folks, trying to whip a giant. How big was John Henry?"

"They tell he was the biggest man ever in Virginia."

"Big as me?"

"Maybe not quite. Maybe just stronger."

"Stronger?"

I near about fled before the anger in Rafe Enoch's face.

"Well," I said, "he beat that steam drill. . . ." And I sang:

"John Henry said to his captain,
'A man ain't nothing but a man,

WALK LIKE A MOUNTAIN 195

But before I let that steam drill run me down,
I'll die with my hamper in my hand. . . .' "

"He'd die trying," said Rafe, and his ears looked sort of cocked forward, the way you hear tell elephants do to listen.

"John Henry drove steel that long day through,
The steam drill failed by his side,
The mountains were high, and the sun got low,
John he laid down his hammer and he died. . . ."

"Killed himself a-beating the drill!" Rafe's pumpkin fist banged into his other palm. "Reckon I'd have beat it and lived."

I looked at the place where the pond might could have a drain-off.

"No use thinking on it," said Rafe. "Even if I wanted to, I don't have no hammer twice the size of ordinary."

A drop of rain fell cold on me. I started round the pond.

"Where you going to?" Rafe called, but I never looked back. Stopped by his wigwam-house and put my guitar inside. In the gloom I saw his homemade stool high as a table, his table almost chin high to a natural man, a bed woven of hickory splits and spread with deer and bear skins to be the right bed for Og, King of Bashan, in the Book of Joshua. From next to the door I grabbed a big hickory pole, off some stacked firewood.

"What you reckon to do?" Rafe thundered.

I went to where the slope started. I poked the hickory betwixt two rocks and pried. He laughed, and the rain sprinkled down.

"Go on, John, grub you out a sluiceway," he granted me. "I enjoy to watch haggly little men work. Come in the house, Page, we can watch from in there."

I couldn't budge the rocks apart. They were as big

as trunks or grain sacks, they must have weighed half-tons. They set in there, one next another, four-five of them holding the water back from spilling down that slope. I heaved on my hickory till it bent like a bow.

"Come on," said Rafe again, and I looked round in time to see his shovelly hand take her by the wrist. Gentlemen, the way she slapped his beardy face with her other hand, it made me jump with the crack.

I watched, knee-deep in water. His hand went to his gold-bearded cheek. His eye-whites glittered in the rain. "If you was a man," he boomed down at her, "I'd slap you dead on this ground."

"Do it," she blazed him back. "I'm a woman, and I don't fear nary overgrown, sorry-for-himself giant ever drew breath!"

With me standing far off enough to forget how little I was by them, they didn't look too far apart in size. Page was like a small-made woman facing up to a sizable man, that was all.

"I'm no man, nor neither are you a man!" she said. "Don't know if you're an ape or a bull-brute or what, but you're no man. John's the only man here and I'm a-helping him. Stop me if you dare!"

She ran to where I was. Rain beat her hair into a brown tumble and soaked her dress snug to her fine proud strong body. Into the water she splashed.

"Let me pry," and she grabbed the hickory pole. "I'll pry up and you tug, and maybe—"

I bent to grab the rock with my hands. Together we strove. Seemed the rock stirred a mite, like the drowsy sleeper in the old song. Dragging at it, I felt my muscles crack and strain.

"Look out!" squealed Page. "Here he comes!"

Up on the bank she jumped again, the hickory ready to club him. He paid her no mind, he stooped down at me.

"Get on out of there!" he bellowed, the way I'd always reckoned a buffalo bull would sound. "Get out, John!"

"No, Rafe," I wheezed. "Got to move this rock—"

"You ain't budging it ary mite!" he near about deafened me in the ear. "Let somebody there can do something!"

He grabbed my arm and snatched me out of the water, so quick I near about sprained my fingers turning loose of the rock. Next second he splashed in, like a tree felled from a bank. His big shovelly hands clamped the sides of the rock, and through the falling rain I saw Rafe Enoch put his man on it.

He swoll up like a mad toad-frog. His patchy fur shirt split down his back while those muscles humped under his hide. His teeth flashed out in his beard, hard set together.

Then, just when I thought he'd bust open, that rock came out of its bed, came up and landed on the bank away from where it had been.

"I swear, Rafe—" I began to say.

"Help him," Page told me. "Let's both help."

We tried to take hold on the next rock, but Rafe hollered us away, so loud we jumped back like scared dogs. That rock quivered, and cracks ran through the rain-soaked dirt round it. Then it came up on end, the way you'd reckon it had hinges, and Rafe got both arms round it and heaved it clear. He laughed, and the rain wet his beard.

Standing back away, Page pointed to the falls' top.

Looked as if the rain hadn't had to put down but just a little bit. Those loose rocks trembled and moved in their places. They were ready to go over. Rafe saw what we saw.

"Run, you two!" he howled above the racketty storm. "Run, run, quick!"

I never tarried to ask the reason. I grabbed Page's arm and we ran for the falls. Running, I looked back past my elbow.

Rafe had stood up straight, straddling amongst the rocks by the slope. He looked at the clouds, that were down almost on his sopping head, and both his big arms lifted and his hands spread and their fingers snapped—*Whop! Whop!* like two pistol shots.

He got what he called for.

A forked stroke of lightning came down on him, straight and hard, like a fish-gig in the hands of the Lord's top angel. It slammed on Rafe and over and around him, and it shook itself all the way from the rocks to the clouds. Rafe Enoch in its grip lighted up and glowed, like a giant forge, hammered out of iron and heated in the sevenfold furnace of Nebuchadnezzar.

I heard the almightiest of tearing noises. I felt the rock shelf quiver all the way to where we stood dead and watched. My thought was, the falls had torn open to drown Sky Notch.

But the lightning yanked back to where it had come from. It had busted open the sluiceway, and water flooded through and down slope, and Rafe had dropped down and it poured and rushed over him.

"He's struck dead!" I heard Page cry out over the rain.

But Rafe Enoch pushed himself up on his knees, then on his feet, and out of that drain-off rush, somehow staggering up from where the lightning had flung him. His knees wobbled and bucked, but he made them draw straight. He mopped a big muddy hand across his big muddy face.

He walked toward us, slow and dreamy, and by now the rain rushed down instead of fell down. It was like what my old folks used to call a-raining tomcats and hoe handles. I bowed my head to it, and made to pull Page toward Rafe's wigwam; but she wouldn't pull, she held where she was till Rafe came up with us. Then we all three went together into the rain and the wind battering outside.

Rafe and I sat on the big bed, and Page leaned against the stool. Her dress was soaked all against her body, showing how nobly God had made her. She wrung water out of her hair.

"You all right?" she inquired Rafe.

He looked at her. Betwixt the drain-off and the wigwam, the rain had washed off that mud that gaumed him all over. He was wet and clean, with his patchy pelt shirt hanging in soggy rags away from his giant's chest and shoulders.

The lightning had burnt off part of his beard. He lifted a hand to wipe off the wet fluffy ash, and I saw the stripe on his naked arm, on the broad back of his hand, and another stripe just like it on the other arm. Lightning had flowed down both hands and arms and clear down his flanks and legs. I saw the burnt lines on his fringed leggins. It was like a double lash of God's whip.

Page came close to him. Just then he didn't look so out-and-out bigger than she was. She put a long gentle finger on the lightning lash where it striped his right shoulder.

"Does it hurt much?" she asked. "You got some grease I might could put on it?"

He lifted his head, heavy and slow, but didn't meet her look. His eyes were on me. "I lied to you," he said.

"Lied?" I repeated him.

"I did call for that rain. Called for the biggest rain I could think of. Didn't pure down want to kill off them folks in the Notch, but to my notion, if I made it rain and then saved Page up here—"

At last he turned his shamed face to her.

"The others would be gone and forgotten, and there'd be only Page and me." His dark eyes held her green ones. "But I didn't rightly know how she disgusts the very sight of me." His head dropped again. "I feel the nearest to nothing I ever felt."

"You opened the drain-off and saved Sky Notch from your flood," said Page, her voice so gentle you'd never believe it. "You called down the lightning to help you."

"I called down the lightning to kill me," said Rafe. "I never reckoned it wouldn't. I wanted to die. Page, all you got to do is tell me to die now, and I'll—"

"Live, Rafe Enoch," she bade him.

He got up from where he sat, and he stood tall over her.

"Stop pestering yourself when folks look on you," she said, still ever so gentle. "They're just wondered at you, Rafe, what a much of a man you are. Folks were wondered that same way at Saint Christopher, the Giant who carried our Lord Jesus across the river."

"I was too proud," he mumbled. "Proud of my Genesis giant blood, of being one of the sons of God."

"Shoo, Rafe," and her voice was the gentlest yet. "What does the least man in size say when he speaks to God? He says, 'Our Father Who art in heaven.' "

Rafe turned from her, and his great powerful shoulders heaved with a sob.

"You said I could look on you if I had the wish," said Page Jarrett. "And I have the wish to look on you, Rafe."

Back he turned, and bent down, and she rose on her toetips so their faces came together.

The rain stopped, the way you'd think their kiss stopped it. But they never seemed to know, and I picked up my guitar and went out toward the lip of the cliff.

The falls were going strong, but that drain-off had handled enough water so there'd be no washout to drown the folks below. I reckoned the rocks would be the outdoingest slippery rocks ever climbed down by mortal man, and it would take me a long spell of time. Long enough, maybe, for me to think of the right way to tell Mr. Lane Jarrett that he was just before having him a son-in-law of the Genesis giant blood, and after while grandchildren of the same family.

The sun came busting through the clouds and flung them away in chunks to the left and to the right, across the bright blue sky.

NONE WISER FOR THE TRIP

abe Mawks howdied Sol Gentry, cutting up a fat deer in his yard. Sol sliced off enough for a supper and did it up in newspaper for Jabe to carry home, past Morg McGeehee's place that you can see from Sol's gate, and from where you can see Jabe's cabin.

Jabe never got home that day. As if the earth had opened, he was swallowed up. Only that wrapped-up meat lay on the trail in front of Morg's. The high sheriff questioned. Jabe's wife sought but did not find. Some reckoned Jabe to be killed and hid, some told he'd fled off with some woman. Twenty-eight long years died.

When one day Morg hollered from his door: "Jabe Mawks!"

"Where's the meat?" Jabe asked to know. "Where's it gone?"

He looked no older than when last he was there. He wore old wool pants, new checked shirt, broad brown hat he'd worn that other day. "Where's the meat?" he wondered Morg.

Jabe's wife was dead and gone, and he didn't know his children, grown up with children of their own. He just knew he didn't have that deer meat he'd been fetching home for supper.

Science men allow maybe there's a nook in space and time you can stumble in and be lost beyond power to follow or seek, till by chance you stumble out again. But if that's so, Jabe is none wiser for the trip.

Last time I saw him, he talked about that deer meat Sol gave him. "It was prime," he said, "I had my mouth all set for it. Wish we had it now, John, for you and me to eat up. But if twenty-eight years sure enough passed me on my way home, why, they passed me in the blink of an eye."

ON THE HILLS AND EVERYWHERE

("John, the children's done opened their Santa Claus gifts, and I want some hot rations inside them before they start on that store-bought candy you fetched them. So why don't you tell us a Christmas tale while Mother's putting the dinner on the table?"

"Be proud to do so. And this won't be any faraway tale, it happened to neighbor-folks you know.")

You and I and everybody worried our heads about Mr. Absalom Cowand and his fall-out with Mr. Troy Holcomb who neighbors him in the hills above Rebel Creek. Too bad when old friends aren't friends any more. Especially the kind of friend Mr. Absalom can be.

You've been up to his place, I reckon. Only a man with thought in his head and a bone in his back would build and work where Mr. Absalom Cowand does, in the high hills beyond the winding road beyond those lazy creek-bottom patches. He's terraced his fields up and behind his house on the slope, a-growing some of the best-looking corn in this day and time. And nice cows in his barn, and good hogs and chickens in his pens, and money in the bank down yonder at the county seat. Mr. Absalom will feed a hungry neighbor or tend a sick one, saving he's quarreled with them, the way he did with Mr. Troy Holcomb.

("Take a whet out of this jug, John. What for did they quarrel?"

"Over something Mr. Troy said wasn't so, and Mr. Absalom said was. I'll come to that.")

That farm is Mr. Absalom's pride and delight on this earth. Mr. Troy's place next door isn't near so good, though good enough. Mr. Absalom looked over to Mr. Troy's, this day I mention, and grinned in that thicketty beard of his that's like a king's beard in a history-book picture. If it sorrowed him, what he saw, he didn't show it. All that sorrowed him, maybe, was his boy Little Anse—crippled ever since he'd fallen off the wagon and it ran over his legs so he couldn't walk, couldn't crawl, hardly, without the crutches his daddy had made for him.

It was round noon when Mr. Absalom grinned his tiger grin over at Mr. Troy's place, then looked up to study if a few clouds didn't maybe mean weather coming on. He needed the rain from heaven. It wondered him if a certain somebody wasn't witching the rain off from his place. Witches are the meanest folks God ever forgot. Looking up thataway, Mr. Absalom wasn't aware of a man coming till he saw him close in sight above the road's curve, a stranger-fellow with a tool chest on his shoulder. The stranger stopped at the mail box and gave Mr. Absalom good day.

"And good day to you," Mr. Absalom said, a-stroking his beard where it bannered onto his chest. "What can I do for you?"

"It's maybe what I can do for you," the stranger replied him back. "Might could be there's some job here for me."

"Well, now," said Mr. Absalom, relishing the way the stranger looked.

He was near about as tall as Mr. Absalom himself, but no way as thick built, nor as old. Maybe in his thirties, and neat dressed in work clothes, with brown hair combed back. He had a knowledge look in his face, but nothing secret. The shoulder that toted the tool chest was a square, strong shoulder.

"You ain't some jackleg carpenter?" said Mr. Absalom.

"No, sir, I learned my trade young and I learned it right."

"That's bold spoken, friend."

"I just mean I'm skilled."

Those words sounded right and true.

"I like to get out in the country to work," the carpenterman said. "No job too big for me to try, and no job too small."

"Well, now," said Mr. Absalom again, "so happens I've got a strange-like job needs doing."

"And no job too strange," said the carpenter.

Mr. Absalom led him round back, past the chicken run and the hog pen. A path ran there, worn years deep by folks' feet. But, some way past the house, that path was chopped off short.

Betwixt Mr. Absalom's side yard and the next place was a ditch, not wide but deep and strong, with water a-tumbling down from the heights behind. Nobody could call for a plainer mark betwixt two men's places.

"See that there house yonder?" Mr. Absalom pointed with his bearded chin.

"The squared-log place with the shake roof, sir?"

"That there's Troy Holcomb's place."

"Yes, sir?"

"My land," and Mr. Absalom waved a thick arm to show, "terraces back off thataway, and his land off the other direction. We helped each other do the terracing. We were friends."

"The path shows you were friends once," said the carpenter. "The ditch shows you aren't friends any more."

"You just bet your neck we aren't friends any more," said Mr. Absalom, and his beard crawled on his jaw as he set his mouth.

"What's wrong with Troy Holcomb?" inquired the carpenter.

"Oh, nothing. Nothing a silver bullet wouldn't fix." Mr. Absalom pointed downhill. "See the field below the road?"

The carpenter looked. "Seems a good piece of land. Ought to be a nice crop a-growing there."

Mr. Absalom's teeth ground in his beard. "A court of law gave me that there field. Troy Holcomb and I both laid claim to it, and the court said I was in the right. But the corn I planted was blighted to death."

"Been quite a much of blight this season," said the carpenter.

"Sure enough, but down valley, not up here." Mr. Absalom glared his eye toward the house across the ditch. "A curse was put on my field. And who'd have reason to curse it, from some hateful old witch-book or other, but Troy Holcomb? I told him to his face, and he denied the truth of it."

"Naturally he'd deny it," said the carpenter.

(*"Shoo, John, is Mr. Troy Holcomb a witch-man? I never heard that told on him."*

"I just say what Mr. Absalom said. Well.")

"If he was a foot higher, I'd have hit him on top of his head," vowed Mr. Absalom. "We ain't spoken since. And you know what he's done?"

"He dug this ditch." The carpenter looked into the running water. "To show he doesn't want the path to join your place to his any more."

"You've flat got it right," snorted Mr. Absalom. "Did he reckon I'd go there to beg his pardon or the like of that? Do I look to be that kind of puppy-dog?"

"Are you glad, not being friends with him?" the carpenter inquired his own questions, looking into the ditch.

"Ain't studying about that," said Mr. Absalom. "I'm studying to match this here ditch-dig job he did against me. Looky yonder at that there lumber."

The carpenter looked at a stack of posts, a pile of boards.

"He cut me off with a ditch," said Mr. Absalom. "All right, if you want a job, build me a fence along

ON THE HILLS AND EVERYWHERE

this here side of his ditch, from the road down below up to where my backyard line runs." He pointed where. "How long will that take you?"

The carpenter put down his tool chest and did some figuring in his head. Then: "I'll do you something that'll pleasure you by supper time."

"Quick as that?" Mr. Absalom looked at him sharp, for he'd reckoned the fence might could take two-three days to build. "You thought it out to be a little small piece of work, ain't you?"

"No job too big or too small for me," said the carpenter again. "You can tell me if it suits you or not."

"You do my job right, I'll pay you worth your while," Mr. Absalom granted him. "I'm a-heading up to my far corn patch. Before sundown I'll come to look." He started off. "But it's got to suit me."

"It'll suit you," the carpenter made promise, and opened the tool chest.

Like a lone working man will do, he started out to whistle.

His whistling carried all the way to Mr. Absalom's house. And inside, on the front-room couch, lay Little Anse Cowand.

You know how Little Anse could hardly stand on his poor swunk up legs, even with crutches. It was pitiful to see him scuff a crutch out, then the other, then lean on them and swing his feet between. He'd scuff and swing again, inching along. But Little Anse never pitied himself. He was cheerful-minded, a-laughing at what trifles he could find to play with. Mr. Absalom had had him to one doctor after another, and none could bid him hope. They allowed Little Anse was crippled for life.

When Little Anse heard the carpenter a-whistling, he upped his ears to hear more. He worked his legs off the couch, and sat up and hoisted himself on his crutches. He crutched and scuffed to the door, and out in the yard, and along the path, following that tune.

It took him a time to get to where the carpenter was working. When he got there he smiled, and the carpenter smiled back.

"What you doing, sir?" Little Anse asked.

"Something to help your daddy out."

"Can I watch?"

"You're right welcome to watch."

"How tall are you, sir?" Little Anse inquired him next.

"Just exactly six feet," the carpenter said.

("Now hold on, John, that's foolish for the lack of sense. Ain't no mortal man on this earth exactly six foot tall."

"I'm telling you what the stranger said."

"But the only one who was exactly six foot—"

"Hold your tater while I tell about it.")

Then Little Anse said, "I relish that song you were a-whistling, Mr. Carpenter. I know some of the words." And he sang a verse of it:

> "I was a powerful sinner,
> I sinned both night and day,
> Until I heard the preacher,
> And he taught me how to pray."

And the chorus:

> "Go tell it on the mountain,
> Tell it on the hills and everywhere. . . ."

"Can I help you?" Little Anse asked when he'd done singing.

"You might could hand me my tools."

By then they felt as good friends as if they'd been knowing each other for long years. Little Anse sat by the tool chest and searched out the tools as the carpenter called for them. There was a tale to go with each one. Like this: "Let me have the saw."

As he sawed, the carpenter explained how, before ary man knew a saw's use, there was a saw shape in the shark's mouth down in the ocean sea, with teeth lined up like a saw's teeth; which may show how some folks allow the animals were wise before the folks were.

"Now give me the hammer, Little Anse."

Pounding nails, the carpenter told of a nation of folks in Europe, who used to believe in somebody named Thor, who could fling his hammer over the mountains and knock out the thunder and lightning.

And he talked about what folks believe about wood. How some knock on wood to keep off bad luck. How the ancient folks, lifetimes back, reckoned spirits lived in trees, good spirits in one tree and bad spirits in another. And how a staff of white thorn is supposed to scare evil off from you.

"Are those things the truth, Mr. Carpenter?"

"Folks took them for truth once. Must be some truth in ary belief, to start it out."

"An outlander showed me a prayer book once, Mr. Carpenter. Read to me from it, how Satan overcame because of the wood. What did he mean by that?"

"He must have meant the Tree of Knowledge in the Garden of Eden. You recollect how Adam and Eve ate of the tree when Satan tempted them?"

"Yes, sir," Little Anse replied him, for, with not much else to do, he'd read the Bible a many times.

"There's more to that outlander's prayer," the carpenter added on. "If Satan overcame by that wood, he was overcome by another wood."

"That must mean another kind of tree, Mr. Carpenter."

"Sure enough it was, Little Anse."

Little Anse was as happy as a dog at a fish fry. It was like school, only in school you get wishing the bell would ring and turn you loose. Little Anse didn't want to be anywhere but just there, a-handing the tools and a-hearing the talk.

"How come you to know so much?" he asked the carpenter.

"I travel in my work, Little Anse."

Little Anse looked over to Mr. Troy Holcomb's yard. "I don't agree in my mind that Mr. Troy's a witch," he said. "If he had power, he'd long ago have cured my legs. Mr. Troy's a nice old man, for all he and my daddy fussed betwixt themselves."

"Tell your daddy that sometime."

"He wouldn't hark. You near about through?"

"All through, Little Anse."

It was getting on for supper time. The carpenter packed up his tools and started with Little Anse toward the house. Moving slow, the way you do with a cripple along, they hadn't gone more than a few yards when they met Mr. Absalom.

"Finished up, huh?" asked Mr. Absalom, then looked. "Well, bless us one and all!" he yelled.

"Wouldn't you call that a good bridge, Daddy?" Little Anse asked.

For the carpenter had driven some posts straight up in the ditch, and spiked others on for cross timbers. On those he'd laid a bridge floor from side to side. It wasn't fancy, but it looked solid to last till Judgment Day, mending the cutoff of the path.

"But I told you I wanted—" Mr. Absalom began to say.

Just then Mr. Troy Holcomb came across the bridge. He's a low-built man, with a white hangy-down moustache and a face as brown as old harness leather. He came over and put out his skinny hand, and it shook like in a wind.

"Absalom," he said, choking in his throat, "you don't know how I been wanting this chance to ask your humble pardon."

Mr. Absalom quick put out his big hand and took that skinny one.

"You done made me so savage mad, telling that I was a witch-man," Mr. Troy said. "If you'd have let me talk, I'd told you the blight was on my downhill corn, too. It only spared the uphill patches. You can come right now and look."

"Troy, I don't need to look," Mr. Absalom made out to reply him. "Your word's as good to me as the yellow gold. I never rightly thought you done any witch-stuff, not even when I said it to you."

"I'm so dog-sorrowed I dug this here ditch," Mr. Troy went on. "I hated it, right with the spade in my hand. Ain't my nature to be spiteful, Absalom."

"No. Troy, nary drop of spite blood in you."

"But you've built this here bridge, to show you never favored my cutting us off from one another—"

Mr. Troy stopped and wiped his brown face with the hand Mr. Absalom didn't have hold of.

"Troy," said Mr. Absalom, "I'm just as glad as you are about that there bridge. But don't credit me with the idea. This carpenter here, he done thought it up."

"And I'll be going," spoke up the carpenter in his quiet way.

They both looked on him. He'd hoisted his tool chest up on his shoulder again, and he smiled at them, and down at Little Anse. He put his hand on Little Anse's head, just half a second of time.

"Fling away those crutches," he said. "You won't need them ever again."

All at once quick, Little Anse flung the crutches from him, left and right. He stood up straight and strong. Then, fast as a boy ever ran on this earth, he ran to his daddy.

The carpenter was gone. The place he'd stood at was empty.

But, looking where he'd been, they weren't frightened, the way they'd be at a haunt or a devil-thing.

For they all at once knew, all three of them, Who the carpenter was and how He's always with us, the way He promised us in the far-back times; and how He'll do whatever job He can, if it will bring peace on earth and good will to men, among nations or just among neighbors.

It was Little Anse who remembered the whole chorus of the song—

("Shoo, John, I know that there song, too! We sang it last night at church for Christmas Eve!"

"I know it too, John!"

"Me, too, I know it!"

"All right then, why don't we sing it together?

"Go tell it on the mountain,
Tell it on the hills and everywhere,
Go tell it on the mountain
That Jesus Christ was born!")

NARY SPELL

Fifty of us paid a dollar to be in the Walnut Gap beef shoot, and Deputy Noble set the target, a two-inch diamond cut in white paper on a black-charred board, and a cross marked in the diamond for us to try at from sixty steps away.

All reckoned first choice of beef quarters was betwixt Niles Lashly and Eby Coffle. Niles aimed, and we knew he'd loaded a bat's heart and liver in with his bullet. Bang!

Deputy Noble went to look. "Drove the cross," he hollered us. "The up-and-down-mark, just above the sideways one."

Then Eby. He'd dug a skull from an old burying ground and poured lead through the eye-hole into his bullet mold. Bang!

Deputy Noble looked and hollered: "Drove the cross, too, just under that there line-joining."

Eby and Niles fussed over who'd won, while I took my turn, with Luns Lamar's borrowed rifle. Bang! Deputy Noble looked, and looked again.

"John's drove the cross plumb center!" he yelled. "Right where them two lines cross, betwixt the other two best shots!"

Niles and Eby bug-eyed at me. "Whatever was your spell, John?" they wondered to know.

"Nary spell," I said. "But in the army I was the foremost shot in my regiment, foremost shot in my brigade, foremost shot in my division. Preacher Ricks, won't you cut up this quarter of beef for whoever's families need it most round Walnut Gap?"

NINE YARDS OF OTHER CLOTH

High up that almighty steepy rock slope with the sun just sunk, I turned as I knelt by my little campfire. Down slope and down to where the river crawled snaky in the valley bottom, I saw her little black shadow splash across the shallow ford I'd found an hour back. At noontime I'd looked from the mountain yonder across the valley and I'd seen her then, too, on another height I'd left behind. And I'd recollected a song with my name in it:

> "On yonder hill there stands a creature,
> Who she is I do not know . . .
> Oh no, John, no, John, no! . . ."

But I knew she was Evadare. I'd fled from before her pretty face as I'd never fled from a living thing, not from evil spell-sayers, nor murder-doers, nor either my country's enemies when I'd soldiered in foreign parts and seen battle as Joshua tells it in the Bible, confused noises and garments rolled in blood. Since dawn I'd run from Evadare, and still she followed, clinging along the trail I'd tried not to leave, toward the smoke of the fire I'd built before I knew she was still after me.

No getaway from her now, for night was a-coming on the world, and to climb higher would be to fall from some steep hidden place. I could wait where I was or I could head down and face her. Wondering which to do, I thought of how we'd first come on each other in Hosea's Hollow.

I don't rightly know how I'd wandered there. Good-sensed men and women try to stay out of Hosea's Hollow, wish it was a lost hollow, wished they couldn't think about it.

Not even the old Indians had relished to go there. When the white folks ran the Indians off, the Indians grinned over their shoulders as they went, calling out how Kalu would give white men the same hard time he'd given Indians.

Kalu. The Indian word means a bone. Why Kalu was named that nobody knew, for nobody who saw him lived to tell how he looked. He came from his place when he was mad or just hungry. Who he met he snatched away, to eat or worse than eat. The folks who'd stolen the Indians' country near about loaded their wagons to go the way they'd come. Then—this was before the time of the oldest man I'd heard tell the tale—young Hosea Palmer said he'd take Kalu's curse away.

Folks hadn't wanted Hosea to try it. Hosea's father was a preacher, he begged him. So did Hosea's mother. So did a girl who'd dreamt to marry Hosea. They said if Hosea went where Kalu denned he'd never come back, but Hosea allowed that good can overcome evil. He went in the hollow, and sure enough he didn't come out but no more did Kalu, from that day on. Both vanished from folks' sight and knowledge, and folks named the place Hosea's Hollow, and nary path led there.

How I came to that hollow, the first soul in long years, it wondered me. What outside had been the broad open light of the day was cloudy grayness there among funny-looking trees. Somewhere I heard an owl hoot, not waiting for night. Likewise I half-heard music, and it came to me that was why I'd walked there without meaning to.

Later, while I watched Evadare climb up trail to

me, I thought how, in Hosea's Hollow, I'd recollected hearing the sure enough music, two days before and forty-fifty miles off.

At Haynie's Fork, hunters had shot a wild hog that belonged to nobody, and butched it up while the lady-folks baked pones of corn bread and sliced up coleslaw, and from here and yonder came folks with jugs of beady white blockader whiskey and music instruments. I was there, too: I enjoy to give aid at such doings. We ate and drank and danced, and the skilledest men gave us music. Obray Ramsey picked his banjo and sang *O where is pretty Polly, O yonder she stands, with rings on the fingers of her lily-white hands*, on to the last verse that's near about the frighteningest last verse ary song has. Then they devilled me to play my silver-strung guitar and give them *Vandy, Vandy* and *The Little Black Train*. That led to tale-telling, and one tale was of Hosea's Hollow and fifty different guesses of what might could have gone with Hosea Palmer and whatever bore the name of Kalu. Then Byard Ray fiddled his possible best, with none of us ever hoping to hear better.

But a tall thin stranger with a chin like a skinny fist and sooty colored hair was there. When Byard Ray had done, the stranger took from a bag a shiny black fiddle. I offered to pick guitar to harmony with him, but he said, "No, I thank you." Alone he fiddled, and, gentlemen, he purely fiddled better than Byard Ray. When he'd done I inquired him his name.

"Shull Cobart," he said. "You're John, is that right? We might could meet again, John."

His smile was no way friendly as he walked off, while folks swore no living soul could fiddle Byard Ray down without some powerful music-secret. That had been two days before, and then I was in Hosea's Hollow, seeming to hear music that was some way like the music of Shull Cobart's black fiddle.

The gray air shimmered, but not the least hot or bright, there where owls hooted by day. I looked on a funny-growing tree, and such flowers it had as I'd not seen before. Maybe they grew from the tree, maybe from a vine a-scrabbling up. They were cup-shaped and shiny black, like new shoes—or like Shull Cobart's shiny-black fiddle, and I felt I heard him still play, saw him still grin.

Was that why I half-heard the ghost of his music, why I'd come to that black-flowered tree in the shimmery gray air? Anyway, I'd found a trail, showing that something moved in Hosea's Hollow, betwixt trees so close-grown each side you wondered could you put a knife among them. I walked the trail, and the gray shimmer seemed to slow me as I walked.

That tune in my head; I swung my guitar round from where it hung with my soogin sack and blanket roll, and tweaked the tune from the silver strings. The shimmer dulled off, or anyhow I moved faster, picking up my feet to my own playing, round a curve bunched with more black flowers. And there, by the trees at one side, was a grave.

Years old it must be, for vines and scrub grew on it. A wooden cross showed it was sure enough a grave. The straight stick was as tall as my chin and as big around as my arm, and the crosspiece wasn't nailed or tied on, it grew on. I stopped.

You've seen branches grown to one another like that—two sorts of wood. The straightup piece was darker than the crosspiece. But both pieces looked alive, though the ends had been cut or broken so long back the raw was gone and the splinters rubbed off. Little bitty twigs sprouted, with broad light-green leaves on the crosspiece and narrow dark leaves on the straight pole. Roots reached into the grave to sprout the cross. And letters were cut on, shaky and deep-dug and different sizes:

PRAy
foR
HosEA PALMeR

NINE YARDS OF OTHER CLOTH 221

So here was where he'd lain down the last time, and some friend had buried him, with word to pray for him. Standing alone in that unchanciness, I did what the cross bade me. In my heart I prayed, *O Lord, let the good man rest as he's earned the right, and when it's my time, O Lord, let me rest as I've earned the right; and bless the kind soul who made and marked a long home for Hosea Palmer, amen.*

While always my hands picked that inner-heard tune, slow and quiet like a hymn. Still picking, I strolled round another curve, and there before me was a cabin.

I reckoned one main room with clay chinking, with a split-plank door on leather hinges and a window curtained with tanned hide. A shed-roofed leanto was tacked at the left, and it and the main cabin had shake shingles pegged on.

The door opened, and I popped behind a tree as a girl came out.

Small-made; yet you saw she was grown and you saw she was proud, though the color was faded from her cotton dress till it was gray as a dove. Her bright sun-colored hair was tied behind her neck with a blue ribbon. She had a rusty old axe, walking proud toward a skimpy woodpile, and on her feet were flat home-made shoes with the hair still on the cowhide. The axe was wobble-handed, but she had strength in her little round arms. She made the axe chew the wood into pieces enough for an armful, carried the wood back into the cabin, and came out again with an old hoe on her shoulder.

From the dug well she drew the bucket. It was old, too, with a couple of silvery trickles leaking out. She dipped a drink with a gourd dipper and dropped the bucket back. Then she went to a cleared patch past the cabin and leaned on the hoe to look at the plants growing.

There was shin-high corn, and cabbages. She studied them, and her face was lovely. I saw that she yearned for her little crop to be food for her. She began to chop the ground along a row, and I slid off down trail again, past the grave, to where I heard water a-talking to itself.

I found a way through the trees, lay down and took a big drink, and washed my face and hands. I put my gear on a flat rock, unlaced my shoes and let the water wash my feet. Then I cut a pole, tied on a string and a hook and baited it with a scrap of smoke meat.

The fishing was good. Gentlemen, fresh fish are pretty things, they show you the cause for the names they've earned—shiner, sunfish, rainbow trout. Not that I caught any such, but what I caught was all right. When I had six I opened my knife to gut them, and built a fire and propped a stone next it to fry meat on and then a couple of fish for supper. They ate good, just as the sun went down across the funny-looking trees, and I wondered if the bright-haired girl had a plenty to eat.

Finally, in the last dim light, I took my handaxe and chopped as much dry wood as I could tote. I wrapped the four other fish in leaves. I slung on my guitar, for I never walk off from that. Back I went up trail to the cabin. Firelight danced in the window as I sneaked through the dooryard and bent to stack the wood by the door log and lay the fish on top of it.

"What are you doing here?"

She ripped the door open, and she had the axe in her hand. I jumped quick away before she could swing that axe.

She stood with feet apart and elbows square, to fill as much of the door as her small self could. Her hair was down on her shoulders, and shone like gold fire from the light inside.

"Oh," she said, and let the axe sink. "You're not—"

"I'm not who?" I inquired her, trying hard to sound laughy.

She leaned tired on her axe. "Not Shull Cobart," she said.

"No, ma'am. You can say for me I'm not Shull Cobart, nor I wouldn't care to be. I saw him one time, and I'm honest to say he doesn't suit me." I pointed to what I'd fetched. "I'm camped yonder by the branch. Had more fish and wood than I needed, thought you might could use them." I bowed to her. "Good night, ma'am."

"Wait." There was a plea to that, and I waited. "What brought you here, Mr.—"

"I'm named John. I just roamed here, without thought of why."

"I'm wondered, Mr.—"

"John," I named myself again.

"I'm wondered if you're the John I hear tell of, with a silver-strung guitar."

"Why," I said, "I'd not be amazed if I had the only silver-strung guitar there is. Nobody these days strings with silver but me."

"Then I hear you're a good man." She looked down at the wood and fish. "Have you had your supper?"

She picked up a fish. "I've not eaten. If you'd maybe like some coffee—"

"Coffee," I repeated her. "I'd relish a cup."

She took the rest of the fish. "Come in, John," she bade me, and I gathered the wood in my arms and walked in after her.

"My name's Evadare," she told me.

The cabin's inside was what I'd expect from the outside. Chinked walls, a stone fireplace with wood burning in it, a table home-pegged together, two stools made of split chunks with branches for legs. In a corner was a pallet bed, made with two old patchy quilts. A mirror was stuck to the wall chinking—a woman purely has to have a mirror. Evadare took a fire-splinter from the hearth and lighted a candle stuck on the table in its own tallow. The glow showed me how pinky-soft her skin was, how young and pretty;

and bigger, bluer eyes than Evadare's you wouldn't call for. At last she smiled, a little hopeful smile.

I wooded up the fire, found a skillet and a chunk of fat meat. I rolled two fish in cornmeal and put them to fry. She poured coffee from a tin pot into two tin cups, and the pot-bottom was sooted as black as Shull Cobart's hair.

When the fish were done I forked them on to an old white plate for her. She ate, and she was hungry. Again she smiled that little small smile, and filled my cup again.

"I'd not expected visitors in Hosea's Hollow," she said.

"You expected Shull Cobart," I said. "You said so."

"He'd come if anybody came, John."

"But he didn't, and I did. Do you care to talk about it?"

She'd done weaving for Shull Cobart, with maybe nineteen others, in a little hill town. He sold the cloth at Asheville at a high mark, to the touristers that come there. Once or twice he made to court Evadare, but she paid him no mind. Then one day he went on a trip, and came back with his black fiddle.

"And he was different," she said. "Before that, he'd been polite to folks. But the fiddle changed him. He played at dances, and folks danced high and fast, but his music scared them, even when they flocked to it. He'd stand by the shop door and play to us girls, and the cloth we wove was more cloth and better cloth— but it had a funny feel and a funny look to it."

"Did the touristers buy it?" I inquired her.

"Yes, and paid more for it, but folks who saw told me they acted scared while they bought it."

"And you ran off from Shull Cobart."

"That was when he said he wanted me to light his darkness."

I could hear an evil man saying those words to a good girl, with his evil hungry for her good. "What did you reply him?"

"I said I wanted to be quiet and good, he wanted to be showy and scary. And he said that was just his reason, he wanted me for my goodness to his scaryness." She shivered, as if ice had fallen outside the window. "I swore I'd go where he couldn't follow. Then he played his fiddle, it somehow bound me hand and foot, I felt he'd tole me off with him then and there, but I pretended—"

She looked sad ashamed of pretending, even in peril.

"I said I'd go with him next day. He waited. That night I ran."

"You ran to Hosea's Hollow," I said. "How did you dare to?"

"I feared Kalu another sight less than I fear Shull Cobart," she told me. "And I've not seen Kalu. I've seen nothing. Heard a couple things, though. Once a knock at the door at night."

"What did the knocking, Evadare?"

"I wasn't so big a fool that I went to see." She shivered again, from her little toes up to her bright hair. "I dragged up the quilt and spoke the strongest prayer I knew, the one about God gives His angels charge over us by day and by night." Her blue eyes were big, recollecting. "Whatever knocked gave one knock more and never again, that night or all nights since."

I was ready to talk of something else. "Who made you this cabin?"

"It was here when I came—empty. But I knew good folks had made it, by the cross."

Her eyes went to the inside of the half-shut door. A cross was cut there. It put me in mind of the grave by the trail.

"Might could be it was Hosea Palmer's cabin. He's dead and buried now. Who buried him?"

She shook her head. "That wonders me, too. Some good friend did it, long years back. Sometimes, when I reckon maybe it's a Sunday, I pray by that grave and sing a hymn. It seems brighter when I sing and look up in the sky."

"Let me guess what you sing, Evadare."

I touched the guitar, and both of us sang it:

> "Lights in the valley outshine the sun,
> Look away beyond the blue. . . ."

As she sang I thought in my heart—how pretty her voice, how sweet the words in her mouth.

She went on to tell how she lived. She'd fetched in meal and salt and not much else, and she stretched it by picking wild greens, and there were some nuts poked away in little handfuls, here and there round the cabin, like squirrels' work; though neither of us had seen a squirrel in Hosea's Hollow. She'd planted cabbages and seed corn, and reckoned these would be worth eating by deep summer. She was made up in her mind to stay where she was till she got some notion that Shull Cobart didn't lie in wait for her outside.

"He's waiting," she felt sure. "He laughed when I said I'd run. Allowed he'd known all I tried to do, all he needed was to wonder a thing while he played his fiddle, and the answer came in his mind." Her little pink tongue wet her lips. "He played one song to have power—"

"Might could it be this?" I tried to jolly her, and again I touched the strings. I sang old words to Shull Cobart's music:

> "My pretty little pink, I once did think
> That you and I would marry,
> But now I've lost all hope of you,
> And I've no time to tarry.
> I'll take my sack up on my back,
> My rifle on my shoulder,
> And I'll go off to the Western States
> To view the country over. . . ."

"That's the tune," she said, "but not the words." Again a shiver. "They were like a dream, while he played and sang along, and I felt all trapped and tangled and webbed."

"Like a dream," I repeated her, and made up words like another thing I'd once heard to fit the same music:

> "I dreamt last night of my true love
> All in my arms I had her,
> And her locks of hair, all long and fair,
> Hung round me like a shadow. . . ."

"That's not his song, either," said Evadare.

"No, it's not," a voice I'd heard before agreed her. In through the half-open door stepped Shull Cobart, with his sooty hair and grin, and the shiny black fiddle in his hand.

"Why don't you bid me welcome?" he asked Evadare, and cut his eyes across to me. "John, I counted on you being here, too."

Quick I leaned my guitar to the wall and got up. "Then you counted on trouble with me," I said. "Lay aside that fiddle, so I won't break it when I break you."

But it was to his chin, and the bow across. "Hark before we fight," he said, and gentlemen, hush! How Shull Cobart could play.

It was the same tune, fiddled beyond my poor tongue's power to tell how wild and lovely. And the cabin that had red-gold light from the fire, and soft-gold light from Evadare's hair, it looked that quick to glow silvery pale, in jumping throbbing sweeps as he played. Once, on a clear cold dry winter night, I saw in the sky the Northern Lights; and in that cabin the air beat and throbbed the same way, but pale silver, I say, not warm red. And it came to my mind, harking helpless, that the air turned cold all at once, like that winter night I'd watched the Northern Lights dance the sky.

Somehow, to come at Shull Cobart was like moving neckdeep against a flooding river. I couldn't wear my way to him. I sat on the stool again, and he stripped his teeth, grinning above me like a dog above a trapped rabbit.

"I wish you the best, John," he said through the music. "See how I make you welcome here."

I knew it wouldn't help to get up again, so I took back my guitar and sat quiet. I looked him up and down. He wore a dark suit with a red stripe, a suit that looked worth money, and his shoes were as shiny as his fiddle. His mean dark eyes, close together above his spell-casting music, read my thoughts inside me.

"Yes, John, it's good cloth," he said. "My own weave."

"I know how it was woven," Evadare barely whispered. She'd moved halfway to a corner. Scared white, but she was a prettier thing than ever I'd seen in my life.

"Want me to weave for you?" he mocked me; and sang a few words to his tune:

"I wove this suit and I cut this suit,
And I put this suit right on,
And I'll weave nine yards of other cloth
To make a suit for John. . . ."

"Nine yards," I repeated him.

"Would that be enough fine cloth for your suit?" he grinned across the droning fiddle. "You're long and tall, a right much of a man—"

"Nobody needs nine yards but for one kind of suit," I kept on figuring, "and that's nary suit at all."

"A shroud," said Evadare, barely making herself heard; and how he laughed at her wide eyes and the fright in her voice!

"Will there be a grave for John here in Kalu's home place, Evadare?" he jeered her. "Would Kalu leave enough of John to be worth the burying? I know about old Barebones Kalu."

"He's not hereabouts," Evadare half begged to be believed. "Not once he's bothered me."

"Might could be he spared you, a-hoping for something better," said Shull. "But he won't spare all of us that came here making a fuss. That's why I toled John here."

"You toled me?" I asked, and he nodded.

"I played you a tune so you'd come, John. I reckoned Kalu would relish you. Being he's what he is, and I'm what I am, it's you he'd prefer. And I'll look after Evadare and take her back."

"I'll not go with you," Evadare said, sharper than I thought possible for her.

"Won't you, though?"

His fiddle music came up, and Evadare drew herself tight, as if she leant back against ropes on her. The music sang itself into wild-sounding notes. Evadare fisted her hands, bit her teeth together, shut her eyes tight. She took a step, or she was dragged. Another step she took, another, nearer to him.

I tried to get up too, but I couldn't move as she moved. I sat and watched, and thought of that saying how a snake draws a bird to his coil. I'd never credited that thing till I saw Evadare move, step by step she didn't want to make, toward Shull Cobart.

Then he stopped playing and breathed hard, like a man who's been a-working in the field. Evadare stood still and trembled. I took up my muscles to make a jump, but Shull pointed his fiddle bow at me like a gun.

"Have sense!" he slung out. "You've both learned I can make you go or stay, which way I will. Sit down, Evadare, and I'll play no more a while. But act foolish, John, and I'll play a note that'll have the bones out of your body without ary bit of help from Kalu."

Bad as he was, he told the truth, and we both knew it. Evadare sat on the other stool and I put my guitar across my knees. Shull Cobart leant on the door jamb, his fiddle low on his chest, and looked sure of himself. I was dead sure that instant I'd never seen among the wicked faces of this earth a wickeder face than his.

"Know where I got this fiddle?" he asked us.

"I can guess," I said, "and it spoils my notion of how good a trader a certain old somebody is. It wasn't much of a swap, that fiddle for your soul; your soul was lost to him before the bargain."

"It was no trade, John." He plucked a fiddle-string with his thumbnail. "Just a little present betwixt friends."

"The fiddle's called the devil's instrument," said Evadare. And once again Shull Cobart laughed at her, then at me.

"Folks have a sight to learn about fiddles. This fiddle will make you and me rich, Evadare. We'll go to the world's big cities, and I'll play the dollars out of folks' pockets and the hearts out of folks' bodies. They'll honor me and they'll bow their faces to the dirt before your feet."

"I won't go with you," she said again.

"Want me to play you right into my arms this minute? Only reason I don't, Evadare—and my arms want you, and that's a fact—I'd have to put down my fiddle to hold you right."

"And I'd be on you and twist your neck round like the stem of a watch," I added onto that. "You know I can do it, and so do I. Any second it's liable to happen."

As he'd picked his fiddle-string, I touched a silver string of my guitar, and it sang like a honey-bee.

"Don't do that, John," he snapped. "Your guitar and my fiddle don't tune together right. I'm a lone player."

To his chin went the shiny black thing, and the music he made lay on me heavy. He sang:

> "I'll weave nine yards of other cloth
> For John to have and keep,
> He'll need that cloth when he lies down,
> To warm him in his sleep. . . ."

"What are we waiting on?" I said. "You might could kill me with your fiddling, but you'll never scare me."

"Kalu will do the scaring," he said, stopping again. "Scare you purely to death. We're just a-waiting on him now."

"How will we know?" began Evadare.

"We'll know," said Shull, like promising a baby child something. "We'll hear him. Then I'll play John out of here to stand face to face with Kalu, if it's really a face Kalu's got."

I laughed, and heaven forgive me the lie I put in my laugh, trying to sound as if naught pestered me. Shull frowned; he didn't like how my laugh hit his ear.

"Just for argument's sake," I said to him, "how do you explain what you say your music does?"

"I don't explain. I just play."

"I've heard tell how a fiddler can be skilled to where he plays a note and breaks a glass window," I said. "I've heard tell he might could possibly play a house to fall down."

"Dogs howl at fiddles," said Evadare. "From pain to their ears."

Shull nodded at us both. "You folks are right. There was power music long times back. Ever hear tell of Orpheus?"

"An old-timey Greek," I said.

"He played his harp, and trees danced for him. He played his way down to the floor of hell and back out again. I might could have got some of that power. A fiddle can sing extra sharp, extra sweet, and it's solid sounding, like a knife or club or rope, if you can work it."

I thought how I'd heard that sound goes in waves like light and can be measured; and a wave is power, whether sound or light. Waves can wash, like the waves of the sea that strike down big walls and strong men. Too bad that educated folks couldn't have that black fiddle, to make its power good and useful. In devil-taught hands, it was the devil's instrument. No way like my guitar strung with silver, the way harps, certain harps in a certain high place, are said to be strung with gold. . . .

Shull was harking. "Something's out yonder," he said.

I heard, too. Not a step or scramble, but anyway a movement.

"Kalu," said Evadare, her blues eyes widest yet in the firelight.

"I reckon so," said Shull. "John, wouldn't it be kindlier to the lady to meet him outside?"

"Much kindlier," I agreed him, and got up.

"You know this isn't personal, John," said Shull, fiddle to his chin. "But Kalu's bound to have somebody. Not Evadare, for in some way he's let her be. And not me, with you here. You've got a name, John, for fighting against things Kalu stands to represent. He'll want a good thing, because he's got a plenty of strong evil."

"The way you think you've got to have Evadare," I said.

"That's it. And you're in the line of what he seeks to devour." He started to play. "Come on, John."

I was a-coming. I'd made up my mind. The pull of the music was on me again. Shull Cobart walked out, fiddling. I winked at Evadare, as if to say it was all right. Then I walked out, too.

The light was greeny-pale, but I saw nary moon.

Maybe the trees hid it, or either the haze in the sky.

"Where will you face him?" asked Shull, almost polite above his playing.

"There's a grave down yonder."

"Sure enough, just the place. Come on."

I followed after him on the trail. My left hand chorded on my guitar at the neck, my right-hand fingers found the strings. What was it Evadare said? ... *I pray by the grave and sing a hymn. It seems brighter* ...

Why not two kinds of power music?

I picked the tune with Shull, softer than Evadare's whisper. He didn't hear; and, because I followed him like a calf to the slaughter pen, he didn't guess.

Round the bend was the grave, the green light paler round it. Shull stopped. Then I knew Kalu was in the trees above us. Somewhere up there, he made a heaviness in the branches.

"Stand where you want to, John. I vow, you're acting the man."

I moved past him, close to the cross, though there wasn't light to see the name or the prayer.

"Drop that guitar!" Shull howled at me.

For I'd begun to play loud, and I sang to his tune, some words I made up for myself:

"I came to where the pilgrim lay,
   Though he was dead and gone,
And I thought I heard a whisper say,
   'My friend sleeps here alone. . . .' "

"Hush up with that!"

Shull Cobart stopped his fiddle and ran at me. I ducked round the cross, and the second verse:

"Winds may come and thunders roll
 And stormy tempests rise
But my friend sleeps here with a peaceful soul
 And the tears wiped from his eyes. . ."

"Come get him, Kalu!" Shull screamed.

Kalu dropped out of the branches and landed betwixt us.

Gentlemen, you wonder what Kalu was. Bones, mostly—something like man bones, but bigger and thicker, maybe like bear bones, or big ape bones from some far land. And a rotten light from them, so I saw for a moment that the bones weren't empty. Inside the ribs were caged dark puffy things, like guts and lungs and maybe a heart that skipped and wiggled. The skull had a long snout like I can't rightly say what, and in its eye-holes burnt blue-green fire.

Out reached the arm bones.

And the finger bones grabbed Shull Cobart.

I heard Shull Cobart scream out high and shrill, and then Kalu had him, like a bullfrog taking a minnow. And Kalu was up in the branches again. Standing by the grave, tweaking my guitar, I heard the leaves rustle, and after that no more sound from Kalu or either from Shull Cobart.

After while, I walked to where Shull had dropped his black fiddle. I smashed it with my foot and kicked the pieces away.

Walking back to the cabin seemed an hour's time. I stopped at the door.

"No!" moaned Evadare, then she took time to look at me. "John—but—"

"That's twice you took me for Shull Cobart," I said.

"Kalu—"

"Kalu fetched Shull away, not me."

She wondered what to say to that.

"I figured the truth on Kalu and Hosea Palmer, when I went out with Shull," I began to explain her. "All at once quick I knew why Kalu hadn't pestered you. You'll be surprised you didn't guess, too."

"But—" she tried once more.

"Who buried Hosea Palmer, with a cross and a

prayer? What dear friend could he have, when he'd come here alone? Who was left here alive when it was Hosea Palmer's dying day?"

She just shook her head from side to side.

"It was Kalu," I said. "Remember the tale, all of it. Hosea Palmer said good would overcome evil. Folks think Hosea destroyed Kalu, some way or other. But what he did was teach Kalu the good things. They weren't enemies then, they were friends."

"Oh," she said. "Oh."

"Kalu buried Hosea," I said. "He cut Hosea's name, and the prayer. Hosea must have taught Kalu his letters. But how would Shull Cobart understand? It wasn't for us to know, even, not till the last minute. And Kalu took the evil man off to punish him."

I sat in the doorway, my arms around my guitar.

"You can go home again, Evadare," I told her. "Shull Cobart won't vex you again, by word of his mouth or by sight of his face."

She'd been sitting all drawn up, as small as she could make herself. Now she managed to stand.

"Where will you go, John?"

"There's all this wide world for me to go through. I'll view the country over. Goodbye, Evadare, think a kind thought for me once in a while when we're parted."

"Parted?" she said after me, like an echo, and took a step, but not as if she was a-dragging in a web of music. "John. Let me come with you."

I jumped up. "Come with me? You don't want to come with me, Evadare."

"Let me come." Her hand touched my arm, trembling like a bird.

"How could I take you with me? I live hard."

"I've not lived easy, John." She said it soft and sweet and lovely, and my heart ached with what I'd not had time till then to feel for Evadare.

"I don't have a home to take you to," I said.

"Your home's where folks make you welcome, all places you go. You're happy. You have what you need. There's music on the way you walk. John, I want to hear the music. I want to help the song."

I made to laugh such a thought, but I couldn't laugh with my mouth so dry. "You don't know what you say," I told her. "Hark at me, I'm going back to my camp now. I'll be out of here before break of day. Evadare, God bless you and keep you, wherever you go."

"Don't you want me to go with you, John?"

I couldn't dare reply her the sudden truth to that. Make her a wanderer of this earth, too? I went away quick. I heard her call my name behind me, but I didn't turn and look. At my camp again, I sat by my died-out fire, wondering, then wishing, then driving the wish from me.

In the black hour before sunup, I got my stuff together and took out of Hosea's Hollow. I came clear of it as the light rose, and mounted a trail to a high ridge above. Something made me look behind me.

Far down the trail I'd been a-walking on, I saw her.

She leaned on a stick and she carried some sort of bundle—maybe a quilt and what little food she might have. She was a-following after me.

"That fool-headed girl," I said, all alone to myself, and I up and slammed on down the far side of the ridge. It took hours until I crossed the bottom below and mounted up another ridge beyond. On the ridge I'd left behind me, I saw Evadare still on the move to follow, her little shape no great much bigger than a crawling fly. Then's when I thought of that old song:

>"On yonder hill there stands a creature,
> Who she is I do not know,
> I will ask her if she'll marry . . .
> 'Oh, no, John, John, no!. . . .'"

NINE YARDS OF OTHER CLOTH 237

But she didn't stand on that hill, she came on. And I knew who she was. And if I asked her to marry, she wouldn't answer no, and what had I to give a woman who'd marry me?

I told myself I'd show her I meant what talk I'd made. I'd just travel faster than she could, get away from her, let her wear herself out, come to her senses.

The whole rest of that long day I fled from her. I didn't stop to eat, only to drink mouthfuls of water from the streams I crossed. Up the height, down the hollow, through the thicket, over the branch. And in the dusky last end of the day I sat quiet and watched her yet still a-coming, a-leaning on her stick for weariness, and I knew I'd better go back down trail to meet her.

She was at the moment when she'd drop. Only her wish and will had kept her a-going that long. She'd lost her ribbon, and the locks of her hair fell round her like a shadow, if you can figure a bright shadow. Her dress was torn, her face was white it was so tired, and the rocks had cut her shoes all to pieces, and blood seeped out of them.

She couldn't speak ary word. She just sagged into my arms when I held them out to her.

I carried her back up to where I camped. From the spring I fetched her water in my cupped hand, and she drank, and I fetched her more, and again more. Then I pulled off her shoes, and in the spring I washed her poor little cut feet. I put down her quilt and my blanket for her to sit on, with her back to a big rock. I mixed up a pone of cornmeal to bake on a flat stone, and strung a few pieces of meat on a green twig to roast for her. I brought her more water.

"John," she managed at last to speak my name. "John."

"Evadare," I said her name back, and we both smiled at one another, and I came and sat down beside her.

"All right," I said. "I'll cease my wandering. I'll get

a piece of land and put up a cabin. I'll plant a crop for us. I'll hoe the corn and—"

"No such thing, John. No. I'm tired now, so tired— but I'll be all right tomorrow. Let's not cease wandering. Let's wander together. View the country over."

Tears in her eyes—tears in mine. But happy tears, sweet as spring rain, sweet to both of us.

I pulled my guitar to me. "Play me a song," she said.

And I remembered another verse to that old song that fitted Shull Cobart's tune:

"And don't you think she's a pretty little pink,
 And don't you think she's clever,
 And don't you think that she and I
 Could make a match forever?. . . ."

A DELL SCIENCE FICTION SPECIAL

STARDANCE

by

SPIDER and JEANNE ROBINSON

A Hugo and Nebula Award-winning novella, STARDANCE is the story of a dancer whose talent was far too rich for one planet to hold—whose vision left a stunning destiny for the human race.

"A major work, not only as entertainment, but as a literary milestone."—Algis Budrys, *Chicago Sun-Times*.

"Sheer good story telling. From opening tragedy to concluding triumph, this is an imaginative and captivating story."—*Publishers Weekly*

A Dell Book $2.50 (18367-7)

At your local bookstore or use this handy coupon for ordering:

| **Dell** | **DELL BOOKS** STARDANCE $2.50 (18367-7)
P.O. BOX 1000, PINEBROOK, N.J. 07058 |

Please send me the above title. I am enclosing $_____
(please add 75¢ per copy to cover postage and handling). Send check or money order—no cash or C.O.D.'s. Please allow up to 8 weeks for shipment.

Mr/Mrs/Miss _____

Address _____

City _____ State/Zip _____

Dell Bestsellers

- [ ] TO LOVE AGAIN by Danielle Steel $2.50 (18631-5)
- [ ] SECOND GENERATION by Howard Fast $2.75 (17892-4)
- [ ] EVERGREEN by Belva Plain $2.75 (13294-0)
- [ ] AMERICAN CAESAR by William Manchester . . . $3.50 (10413-0)
- [ ] THERE SHOULD HAVE BEEN CASTLES
   by Herman Raucher $2.75 (18500-9)
- [ ] THE FAR ARENA by Richard Ben Sapir $2.75 (12671-1)
- [ ] THE SAVIOR by Marvin Werlin and Mark Werlin . $2.75 (17748-0)
- [ ] SUMMER'S END by Danielle Steel $2.50 (18418-5)
- [ ] SHARKY'S MACHINE by William Diehl $2.50 (18292-1)
- [ ] DOWNRIVER by Peter Collier $2.75 (11830-1)
- [ ] CRY FOR THE STRANGERS by John Saul $2.50 (11869-7)
- [ ] BITTER EDEN by Sharon Salvato $2.75 (10771-7)
- [ ] WILD TIMES by Brian Garfield $2.50 (19457-1)
- [ ] 1407 BROADWAY by Joel Gross $2.50 (12819-6)
- [ ] A SPARROW FALLS by Wilbur Smith $2.75 (17707-3)
- [ ] FOR LOVE AND HONOR by Antonia Van-Loon . . $2.50 (12574-X)
- [ ] COLD IS THE SEA by Edward L. Beach $2.50 (11045-9)
- [ ] TROCADERO by Leslie Waller $2.50 (18613-7)
- [ ] THE BURNING LAND by Emma Drummond $2.50 (10274-X)
- [ ] HOUSE OF GOD by Samuel Shem, M.D. $2.50 (13371-8)
- [ ] SMALL TOWN by Sloan Wilson $2.50 (17474-0)

At your local bookstore or use this handy coupon for ordering:

Dell **DELL BOOKS**
P.O. BOX 1000, PINEBROOK, N.J. 07058

Please send me the books I have checked above. I am enclosing $_____
(please add 75¢ per copy to cover postage and handling). Send check or money
order—no cash or C.O.D.'s. Please allow up to 8 weeks for shipment.

Mr/Mrs/Miss _____

Address _____

City _____ State/Zip _____